This book should be returned to any branch of the
Lancashire County Library on or before the date

Lancashire County Library
Bowran Street
Preston PR1 2UX

Lancashire
County Council

www.lancashire.gov.uk/libraries

Published by Accent Press Ltd 2015

ISBN 9781783752478

Chapter One

Laurel looked up with a smile as the bell over the door heralded a new customer. And the world stopped. She felt her whole body still, could swear that her heart missed a beat or two. Now, at last, she understood what her friends had tried to tell her about lust. She didn't *need* this man, but she *wanted* him.

In the doorway stood the most attractive person she'd ever seen. He was tall and dark, certainly, but not classically handsome. His face was too strong for that. His jaw was firm and his brow straight. His perfectly cut midnight black hair fell back into place again as he ran a hand through it, as though it didn't dare misbehave. Cool grey eyes surveyed the small, busy restaurant, rested on her for a moment, then moved on. She felt a sharp pang of disappointment that the sight of her hadn't affected him in the slightest. Before his glance had brushed over her without a flicker of interest, she'd flirted with the thought that she'd seen her destiny walk through the door.

A diner on her way to the ladies' cloakroom near the entrance gave the man a flirtatious smile. She must have been at least a dozen years too old for him, but it didn't stop her recognising a prime male specimen. His brief smile was cool and cynical. He didn't appear the least bit surprised by the attention.

Laurel laughed and shook her head. This man was way out of her league. His casual sweater was probably cashmere; his trousers well cut, encasing long, lean legs; his leather loafers looked hand made. He carried himself with an assurance that came when people deferred to you

1

and you were confident enough not have to worry about what anybody else thought. She, on the other hand, wore a cheap white blouse and even cheaper black skirt. Her slender legs were encased in dark tights which made her hot and uncomfortable, and her flat black pumps had a hole in one sole. She watched as the stranger surveyed the weekend lunch crowd and wondered what he was doing here.

'Wow! TDH or what?'

Fellow waitress Joanne sidled past, her arms laden with plates of food.

'TDH?' Laurel looked puzzled.

'Tall, dark, and handsome, stupid!'

Amen to that, she thought, although there was no way she would admit it to her friend. She'd never hear the end of it. 'You've got to stop calling the customers stupid,' she teased sternly.

Joanne laughed and delivered her order. Laurel picked up the empty plates from the table she'd been clearing and headed towards the kitchen, her practiced gaze simultaneously checking her other tables to ensure the diners had everything they needed, all the time aware of *his* progress across the room. A few regulars returned her smile, including Florence, her elderly friend, sitting at her usual table.

'Hi, Florence. Been stood up?'

Laurel always enjoyed seeing the old lady, who had taken to eating at the restaurant a couple of times a week. Ever since Laurel had chased off a mugger who had been intent on grabbing Florence's handbag in the street outside, she and older woman had become firm friends. Florence was another person who on the face of it shouldn't be here. The reasonably-priced family restaurant wasn't nearly classy enough for such an elegant lady. But she seemed to like it. And Joanne's partner Chris, who worked in the kitchen, was an excellent cook. Thanks to him the place was getting quite a good reputation. So perhaps a few more up-market types might start coming in.

'No, dear. He's just arrived. I'm looking forward to introducing you. It's such a shame you couldn't join us for a meal.'

Laurel registered the connection between Florence and the stranger at the same moment that they each raised a hand in acknowledgement of the other. *Oh my God! He's her godson?* Somehow, Laurel had had the impression that he should have been much younger. Florence had talked about how he'd spend his school holidays with her, and Laurel had assumed it hadn't been very long ago. Oh, she knew Florence had said he was a successful businessman now, but somehow Laurel hadn't been able to get past the image of the teenage schoolboy the older woman had described with such affection. She assumed some kid had inherited the family business and someone was running it for him. She'd even been a bit jealous, wishing she'd had someone like Florence to stay with instead of a string of foster parents. If she'd thought about an older version of the boy at all, it had been a balding, paunchy fat-cat, not this sleek panther.

For a second, Laurel felt cheated. Knowing who this magnificent stranger was spoilt the thrill she'd experienced when she'd first seen him. She supposed she should have realised the minute he walked in, but ... She shrugged. Anyway, time to get out of Dodge.

She forced herself to turn away as he came closer, so that she wouldn't be tempted to stand and stare. What would he think, Laurel thought uneasily, about her friendship with his godmother?

She trembled as he brushed past her, his hands resting lightly on her shoulders with a murmured apology as he slipped through the space behind her. Unwilling to look at him, she just nodded and smiled at Florence.

'I'll ... er ... be back to get your order in a minute,' she

3

murmured to the old lady.

Shaken by her uncharacteristic reaction to this man, Laurel quickly escaped into the kitchen before the promised introduction could be made.

Unaware of the girl's agitation and focussed on finding his lunch date, Daniel French's frown lifted as he reached the woman sitting regally at a corner table.

'Florence, how are you? Have you been waiting long?' He bent to kiss her paper-thin cheek.

'Hello, darling. No, I've only been here a few minutes. I'm glad you could make it. I know you're so busy these days.'

'Never too busy to have lunch with my favourite godmother,' he smiled, easing his long frame into the seat opposite her.

'I'd be more flattered if I wasn't your *only* godmother,' she responded, her eyes twinkling, giving her a girlish look, despite her perfectly coiffured white hair and the lines on her carefully made-up face, which testified to eight decades of a life lived well.

He laughed and felt himself relax for what seemed like the first time in weeks. He was pleased to see the table was set for just the two of them. Florence had mentioned inviting a friend, but he wasn't in the mood to make small talk with strangers. He'd rather have Florence to himself.

'So, you've decided to spend the winter in Monaco?'

'Yes.' She flexed hands gnarled with arthritis. 'The climate will be better for my old bones. I've had enough of English winters. It was sweet of you to suggest it. Are you sure you won't want to use the apartment yourself?'

He shook his head. 'I've got far too much on over the next few months. I might manage a weekend to check up on you, but it's all yours for as long as you want it.'

'Well, you must make sure you do come when you can. I haven't been to the casino in Monte Carlo for so long, and it's no fun without a handsome man to show off.'

'It's a date,' he smiled. 'Just as soon as I can get away.'

He sighed as his mobile rang. He looked at the caller ID and scowled. Lucy Pemberton again. Would the stupid girl ever leave him alone? 'In fact, it might be sooner rather than later,' he said and switched off the phone.

'Problems?' Florence asked.

He shrugged. 'Possibly.'

'It must be personal. You're never uncertain about business. Woman trouble?'

'Hardly a woman,' he dismissed.

'Oh dear. Is young Lucy still making a nuisance of herself? If she won't take the hint, you really should talk to her father, Daniel. I feel sorry for the girl of course, but it's about time she stopped making a fool of herself.'

'I know.' Why Lucy imagined he'd be interested in a gauche young girl like her he had no idea. He preferred his women to have a measure of sophistication she just didn't possess, despite the expensive finishing school her father had sent her to.

'She's in love with the idea of being in love at the moment,' said Florence. 'But Gerald Pemberton isn't helping matters. He's never given the poor child the chance to learn her own mind, so she's set on you because she knows her father approves. But you're not the right man for her and she's certainly not the right woman for you.'

'There's no such thing as "the right woman" Florence.'

'Nonsense! You're just looking in the wrong direction,' she responded briskly.

'I'm not looking. Full stop,' he said, softening his cynical words with a smile.

'Just because your parents were spectacular failures at marriage, Daniel, doesn't mean you will be. You never fail at anything you set your heart on. Look at what a success you've made of your businesses. But what good is all that money if you don't slow down and enjoy it?'

Before he could respond, Florence's attention was caught by someone standing behind him.

'Ah, Laurel, my dear, there you are. Come and meet my godson.'

Daniel hid a sigh. So the friend had arrived after all. He reluctantly got to his feet. He felt irritated that he had to make polite conversation to a stranger when he wanted to enjoy a quiet lunch with the older woman who had been more like a mother than the woman who had given birth to him. But neither did he want to upset his companion, so he made sure his features reflected polite interest as he turned to come face to face with the blonde woman he'd spotted earlier. His smile widened into a more natural curve and he held out his hand. It wasn't until she fumbled with her notepad and pen that he realised that he was about to shake hands with a waitress.

Caught unawares, he blinked in surprise. A waitress? It made a change from Florence's usual menu of pampered young things looking for a rich husband. This one looked like she should be looking for a good meal. To say she was petite was to be generous. Barely 5'2 and fine boned, she had the ethereal quality of a fairy. The girl looked at him steadily for a moment, her green eyes challenging even as a rosy flush spread from below the collar of her white blouse. Daniel watched in fascination, trying to remember the last time he'd seen a woman blush. After a brief hesitation, she placed her slender hand in his.

He'd seen her as he'd come in, of course. With her blonde hair arranged in a French plait, exposing the elegant line of her jaw and throat, he had been tempted to look back and enjoy the view, but when he had, she'd turned away and he'd caught sight of his godmother waiting for him.

'Laurel, meet Daniel French, my favourite godson.' Florence smiled at him, enjoying the opportunity to turn the joke on him. He was her only godson. 'This is Laurel

Park, Daniel. I was hoping she could join us for lunch today, but she couldn't get the time off.'

The girl disengaged her hand from his and turned her gaze on the older woman, giving her an apologetic smile.

'Sorry, Florence, but we're fully booked today. There was no way.'

Daniel's eyes narrowed as he detected the faintest whiff of relief in her soft voice. She didn't want to join them. Why not? He felt his interest quicken. Or maybe it was his suspicious instincts. This young woman didn't quite fit his perception of one of Florence's close friends. He wanted to know more about her. Purely to ensure that his godmother wasn't being taken for a ride, of course. She was far too trusting, and she wasn't getting any younger. Laurel Park might intrigue him on a physical level, but he would need to know a lot more about her before he trusted her with his beloved godmother.

'Oh well, never mind, dear. We can chat as you serve us. I realise you're busy. Oh, and I've got something for you.' Florence reached for her bag and brought out a leather-bound book.

The girl took the book and opened it to the title page. Her eyes widened, and her generous mouth formed a breathless *'oh!'*

Daniel moved to glance over her shoulder. He resisted the urge to touch her again, but couldn't help breathing in her fresh scent.

'Very nice,' he said, watching the pulse on her throat increase. *'Great Expectations.* An early edition. A very generous gift.'

Laurel stiffened. Florence waved a dismissive hand.

'Nonsense. It's a copy that has been on my bookshelf for years. I've another which has larger print and is much easier for me to read these days. I don't need two, and I know Laurel will enjoy this.'

The girl closed the book carefully, and after the briefest

of pauses offered it back to his godmother.

'Florence, I can't take this. It's ... it's very kind of you, but ...'

'But you love Dickens,' the older woman looked confused.

'I do. But ... I couldn't look after a beautiful book like this. I'm sorry, but I'd be scared to death of losing it, or spoiling it.' She shook her head with what seemed like real regret. 'I really appreciate you wanting to give it to me, but I can't accept it. You've given me so much already.'

Suddenly Daniel's senses were on alert. He was fully aware of his godmother's generous nature. Had this girl been taking advantage? She handed back the book with regret, but was that for his benefit? Would she have taken it if he hadn't been there?

Florence's gentle face was full of compassion as she smiled up at the girl.

'No more than you deserve, child. Now,' she took a deep breath, depositing the book back in her bag. 'We'd better order before you get into trouble. Do sit down, Daniel, dear. I can recommend most of the items on the menu. The chef here is a true artist.'

Laurel had to concentrate hard to get their order down on her pad. Her hand shook as she wrote. The effort of acting normally was a strain. First, Daniel French had thrown her for a loop just by walking into the restaurant, and then he turned out to be Florence's godson! She'd been hearing about him from her elderly friend for weeks – about his homes around the world, his successful businesses, the women who threw themselves at him. But the lifestyle Florence had described was so far removed from her own ordinary life, so out of her league, that she hadn't paid much attention. Consequently she'd managed to build up completely the wrong picture in her mind, focussing instead on the stories of the boy he had been. She hadn't expected the man he really was to make her feel anything like this shaky excitement, this desire to touch and be touched. Her hand felt warm and tingly from just one brief contact. It was crazy! The only thing they had in common was that they both loved Florence.

And the gift! She'd never been given anything so beautiful in her life. Florence had chosen the most perfect thing. It had been special – had made her feel so special. But she couldn't keep it. She ached with regret, but she knew she had done the right thing. A book like that needed to be kept in the right conditions, not stuffed into a cardboard box with her cheap paperbacks and second-hand books. It shamed her that Florence knew and understood. She was one of the few people that Laurel had allowed close enough to see the reality of her life. It still amazed and humbled her that this genteel old lady had managed to get past her usually impenetrable defences. And that she still thought her, Laurel Park, worthy of her friendship.

A quick glance at her friend's companion increased her misery. Gorgeous he may be, and that he was fond of Florence she had no doubt, but she had no illusions about how he saw her. The waitress. Not good enough for such an expensive gift from the older woman. She'd seen the suspicion in his eyes, heard the mockery in his deep, velvet voice. Even if she'd thought she might keep the book, just the look on his face would have persuaded her otherwise. In her short life Laurel had met enough people with the same attitude to recognise Daniel French for the snob he was. He knew nothing about her, and yet he'd judged her already.

At least she knew where she stood. Now if she could just stop her wayward body from wanting to lean against his, she'd be fine. She shivered as she remembered the thrill that had coursed through her when she'd felt his warm breath on her neck as he'd leant close. She needed to keep her distance from this man.

At last she had their order and could escape.

'Isn't she quite lovely, Daniel?' Florence watched her young friend walk away. 'She reminds me of me when I was a girl.'

'No one can ever be as lovely as you,' he declared, unwilling to comment on Laurel Park's charms. 'How long have you known her?'

'Oh, months. She came to my rescue just outside here when some young lout tried to steal my handbag.'

'You were mugged? When?' he asked, appalled. 'Why didn't you tell me?'

'Daniel, dear, calm down. As I said, it was months ago, and Laurel was there within seconds. She made a tremendous fuss, yelling and rushing at the boy.' She smiled as she described how fierce her young friend had been defending her. 'He dropped the bag and ran. It was all quite exciting.'

'Did the police arrest him?'

'He was long gone. There didn't seem much point in calling them. I hadn't lost anything, and no one was hurt.'

Daniel closed his eyes and took a calming breath. The thought of some young thug attacking Florence made his blood run cold. He only hoped it wasn't all part of a more elaborate operation to defraud the old woman.

'I take it your waitress friend was happy to accept a reward for her services?'

'Actually, she keeps on refusing. I've been trying to give her something, anything, but she won't accept. You saw for yourself. She wouldn't even take a book, and I know how she loves them. We met again in the park a few days after the attack. We sat on the same bench, got out our books, and discovered we were both re-reading *Pride and Prejudice.*'

'So she likes to read. What else do you know about her?'

'Enough to have asked her to come to Monaco as my

companion.'

Daniel was unable to hide his alarm. Florence gave him a stern look.

'Don't worry, she turned me down.'

'Why?' he couldn't resist asking, even as he registered a mix of relief and confusion. The girl had been offered the chance of a lifetime to live in luxury, yet she'd failed to take advantage.

'She says she doesn't have a passport.'

'That's hardly a problem. If she wanted to she could get one easily enough.'

'Of course she could. But she has more pride than to take what she regards as charity. She's convinced the job offer is a fake and I'm still trying to give her a reward she doesn't believe she deserves.'

'And she'd be right, of course. You've never needed to employ someone to look after you. You're far too independent.'

'Let's not discuss this with my young friend approaching with our starters, my dear,' she smiled serenely, her warning clear.

Laurel served the soup and whitebait they had ordered. Her smile for Florence was genuine, if a little strained. The blank-eyed expression she turned on Daniel put him firmly in his place.

'Enjoy your meal,' she said, the sentiment as false as the smile she gave him.

'I don't think your friend likes me very much,' he mused as she left.

'Don't take it personally, darling. Laurel doesn't trust easily, and you, my dear, are far beyond her sphere of experience.'

'I don't bite, you know. You make me sound like a monster.'

Florence smiled as he bit into a tiny fish. She was well aware of her godson's reputation as a shark.

'Not at all. In fact, I think you'd be perfect for her, and she for you. She's bright and funny and has a dignity that is rare in someone of her age.'

Daniel groaned. 'Florence, you promised. No more match-making. Especially not with some slip of a girl who you barely know.'

Florence put her spoon down and dabbed at her lips with a napkin. He suspected she was hiding a smile.

'Actually, you've misunderstood,' she gave him her most innocent look. Usually a bad sign. 'I don't want you to romance her, Daniel, I want you to employ her.'

This was a novel approach, even for her.

'I don't have any vacancies for waitresses in my business.'

'No, but as I've just said, Laurel is bright. She's just finished her A-levels, and she needs a chance.'

'A-levels?'

'Yes. English, Law, Business Studies, and French.'

'How old is she?' Good grief, was his godmother trying to get him to adopt her?

'She'll be twenty-three in a couple of months.'

Older than he thought. Which begged another question.

'So why has she only just passed her exams? Resits?'

'Of course not,' Florence, her tone implying that he was a particularly slow child. 'Laurel had to leave school at sixteen, and has been working to support herself ever since. She's studied for years in her spare time, and now she needs to find employment with some prospects.'

'Why can't her family help her?' Daniel was finding this story implausible at the very least. If she was as bright as Florence insisted, why was she relying on her to find her employment? And why did she turn down her offer of a job in Monaco?

Florence went pale, her gaze focussed just beyond his shoulder. Daniel felt the hair stand up on the back of his neck.

'Oh dear,' she said softly.

Daniel looked round to see Laurel behind him, her white face set, her eyes burning. He glanced back at Florence, who suddenly looked every one of her eighty-odd years.

'You promised not to interfere,' the girl accused in a low voice thick with tears. 'You said you believed in me, that I could do it on my own. Now you're turning me into a charity case, begging your big-shot godson to give me a job.'

'I'm sorry, Laurel, dear. I know you can do it. But I'm off to Monaco in a few days for the winter, and I do worry about you. I just wanted to move things along, and I know you'd be such an asset to Daniel. He'd be lucky to have you working for him.'

'That's not the point,' she protested.

Daniel caught his godmother's eye as she put her hands on the table, her head bowed, then pulled herself up to stand. He was concerned for a moment, until she gave him a sly wink before raising her head to face her young friend.

'I know, my dear, and I'm sorrier than you'll know. Please don't be cross with me.' She raised a shaky hand to her temple, and immediately Laurel took the bait.

'Are you all right?'

'I ... I'm fine, my dear. I'm just a little warm. I think I'll go and splash some cold water on my wrists. '

Daniel shook his head, wondering who was scamming who. The old girl should have won an Oscar for that performance. What the hell was she playing at?

Florence left the table and Laurel turned to face him. Her green eyes looked huge, magnified by the sheen of moisture she prevented from falling through sheer will. Pride made her hold his gaze as she gathered up their dishes, finding them by instinct and stacking them without missing a beat.

'Yes, you would be lucky,' she informed him. 'I'm the

hardest worker you'll ever meet, and I'm smarter than most of the shirts you see strolling in here for their liquid lunches on a weekday. But I don't want to work for someone who only takes me on as a favour. I'll find my own job, thanks. Just like I always have. So don't worry, Mr French. You're off the hook.'

He reached out and stayed her hand as she went to pick up the dirty plates.

'Don't take it out on Florence. She's trying to help you because you helped her when she needed it, and because she likes you. If your misplaced pride is so important that you end up hurting her, you're not as clever as you think.'

He wasn't surprised to find his long fingers had wrapped easily around her slender wrist, but he was startled by the strength she used to prise them off and bend his middle finger back until he swore and released her.

'Don't manhandle me, Mr French,' she warned, before she picked up the dishes and stalked off.

He turned in his chair to watch her, his own pride refusing to allow him to acknowledge the throbbing pain in his hand. He wondered how many other men had underestimated her strength and come off worse. He had no doubt that if he'd been standing she would have aimed for a far more sensitive part of his anatomy. He didn't know whether to be mad as hell or laugh as he watched her retreating back, her blonde plait swishing from side to side as she headed quickly towards the kitchen.

She had just reached the kitchen door and turned to push it open with her back when Laurel dropped her load and ran past him towards the front of the restaurant. It took him only a split second to see the lorry, its driver slumped at the wheel, heading straight for the front window, and to see his elderly godmother walking out of the ladies oblivious to the danger.

Time slowed as adrenaline shot through him.

He was out of his seat and sprinting towards her before

he realised that Laurel had the same idea, yelling at people to get out of the way. Everyone moved at once, knocking chairs and glasses over as they scrambled to safety. People were screaming and pushing, panic taking over. Shock seemed to hold Florence frozen as chaos reigned around her. The distance between them was just a few feet, but seemed impossibly far to Daniel as he fought to reach her. He could see Laurel's blonde head ahead of him and realised that they were both too late.

'No!' he cried, fear gripping him as she moved into the path of the lorry as it mounted the kerb. Laurel grabbed Florence and twisted, trying to escape as the entire frontage of the restaurant imploded with a deafening crash.

'Laurel!' he shouted, reaching for them, but not close enough.

'Here!' she yelled as she shoved the older woman towards him with all her strength.

His arms closed around her and he staggered back, watching in horror as Laurel lost her footing and stumbled, her arms reaching out, her face reflecting fear and shock as the runaway lorry caught her a glancing blow and sent her flying through the air.

Chapter Two

Laurel surfaced from unconsciousness slowly, emerging into a world fuzzy with pain. She tried to move into a more comfortable position, only to groan in agony as her body protested.

'Lie still. I'll get someone to give you some pain relief.'

Who was that voice? The deep velvet tones soothed her and she knew she'd heard it before. But where he came from, she had no idea. Before she could open her eyes to check, she heard a door open and close. With a sigh she lay still, trying to figure out where she was and what she was doing there. At first it seemed to hurt everywhere, but as she forced herself to relax and focus she realised that the pain was centred in just a few places.

Her left wrist throbbed. It felt heavy. She knew what that meant. A particularly sadistic foster brother had snapped it when she was fifteen. It was broken again.

Ribs. It hurt like hell to breathe.

Head. Aching. She tried to open her eyes, but one was swollen shut. The right side of her face felt hot and sore.

The room was dimly lit, but with her good eye she could make out the bare lines of a hospital room. Somewhere, out of her line of vision, there must be some flowers, their heady scent masking the usual antiseptic aroma she associated with these places.

The door opened, admitting two men and a woman. A middle-aged man in a suit picked up her notes and started reading them, so he had to be the doctor, and the woman who immediately started checking her pulse was obviously a nurse. The second man stood back, letting the professionals work. Laurel couldn't see him, but knew instinctively he was 'the voice'.

'Good evening. I'm Dr Harding. It's good to see you awake. How are you feeling?'

'Rough,' she whispered through dry lips.

'Much pain?'

'Yeah.'

'Well now that you're awake we can deal with that,' he responded and began giving the nurse instructions.

Laurel allowed them to examine and fuss over her for a few minutes without complaint. She'd suffered worse than this in her life, and had learned early on not to make a noise or show weakness. She was aware of the man leaning against the wall by the door but still couldn't see him. She smiled grimly to herself that her curiosity about the mystery man was at least helping to take her mind off the pain as she was handled and injected.

At last they were finished, and she sighed with relief.

'The medication should start to work in a few minutes. The main thing she needs is rest,' the doctor confirmed as he and the nurse left the room.

Laurel started to frown, but stopped when it hurt. Why were they talking to him, and not her? She watched as he pushed away from the wall and approached the bed. As soon as she got a clear look at his face, she recognised him. The scene at the restaurant flashed into her mind. This was Daniel French. Florence's godson. *Oh dear God!* The only reason he would be here waiting for her to wake up would be to tell her …

'Florence!' she cried, instinctively trying to get up.

Pain exploded across her chest as her bruised ribs protested. Daniel was by her side immediately, pushing her back onto the bed, his big hands gently holding her there as she fought for breath. What the physical pain had been unable to do, the mental anguish now achieved as she gave in and wept.

'I'm sorry. I'm so sorry. I tried to …'

'Hush, Laurel, it's all right. Florence is fine. You saved her.'

'She … she's really OK?' she asked through her tears. 'You promise?'

Daniel sat on the edge of the bed and brushed some wisps of hair away from her forehead.

'I promise. She's sleeping in a room down the hall. She's been sitting right here waiting for you to wake up for hours. The doctor and I had quite a job getting her to rest.'

'A room? What is this place? I thought it was a hospital. You said she was all right.' This was too confusing.

'It is, and she is,' he explained. 'Florence refused to go home until she saw for herself that you were all right, so I arranged for a private room for her so that she could stay close and rest.'

Laurel closed her eye and relaxed, letting the fear flow out of her. Her friend was all right. The combination of relief and the drugs she'd been given were working wonders. She suddenly felt euphoric. The urge to cry again – with happy tears this time – began building up inside her. She sniffed.

'Here, let me …'

The soft stroke of fine cotton on her cheeks as he wiped her tears was almost too much. But she didn't have the will or the energy to turn her head away.

'I never cry,' she whispered.

'Not for yourself, that's for sure,' he confirmed. 'I've seen men twice your size howl like babies over bruised ribs. You only cried when you thought about Florence.'

'And wouldn't you have cried? If she'd …?'

'Died?' Laurel refused to flinch at his angry tone. 'Of course I bloody would! I'm not criticising you, woman.'

'You don't strike me as the type to appreciate women

weeping all over you,' she remarked, her tears drying and tongue loosening as the medication took hold.

He shrugged. 'Normally I'm impatient with females who cry for any little thing. But after the way you got Florence out of the path of that truck – and given the knocks and bruises you sustained doing it – I'm willing to forgive you anything right now.'

'Yeah, right.' She tried to cover how much his words touched her with some street-wise scorn. 'You're going to turn into my fairy godfather and grant me three wishes.'

'For the record I'm definitely *not* a fairy and I've no desire to be anyone's godfather. And I think it was the genie who granted three wishes.'

'I don't know.' She'd never really got into happy-ever-after stories. 'God, can't a girl get away with a tiny bit of sarcasm even when she's lying on her death bed?'

'You're not dying, Laurel. I know it hurts like hell, but you'll be OK.'

She scowled at his amusement.

'I know. But I reckon I'm entitled to a bit of a moan right now.'

'Fair enough,' he conceded. 'You didn't complain earlier, when they were manhandling you. As I said, I've seen grown men cry when a medic has touched injuries like yours.'

Laurel shrugged. The fact that the movement didn't hurt heartened her. She wasn't stupid enough to imagine the pain was gone for ever. As soon as the meds wore off, she'd be lucky to be able to breathe without pain. Maybe they'd give her some on prescription to take away when she went home.

'They had to do it. No point in whining about it. They just take longer and hurt more if you do.'

'Sounds like you have a lot of experience.'

'I've ended up in casualty a time or two. Never in one as posh as this, though.'

'This is a private wing of the hospital.'

Laurel laughed, which turned into a cough.

'Ow! You shouldn't joke. It hurts.'

'No joke.'

'Well, you'd better get them to shift me pretty quick, because there's no way I can pay for this.'

'My treat.'

'No thanks.'

'No thanks required. I chose to do it, and you were in no fit state to have any say in the matter. You're still not.' He sounded bored, as though the discussion was below him. Fine for him – but Laurel didn't have the luxury of being blasé about money.

'I'll pay you back,' she insisted. It might take years, but she would. She hadn't accepted a hand-out since she was sixteen, and wasn't going to now. No matter what, Laurel Park paid her way and was beholden to no one.

'You've already paid,' he said. 'You wouldn't be here if you hadn't gone after Florence. Covering the cost of your medical care is the least I can do.'

'But you don't even know me.' He'd probably have dumped her in casualty and hoped she died if he did.

'I don't need to. I'd do the same for anyone who did what you did today. And if it wasn't me, you'd be having this fight with Florence.'

'I'm not fighting. I'm asserting my independence.'

'Well, give it up for a couple of days, there's a good girl.'

Laurel closed her good eye, unwilling to look at him.

'You really are a patronising bastard, aren't you? Annoying too,'

She heard his soft laugh.

'You'll have to do better than that, Laurel. I've been insulted by professionals.'

'I'm surprised you noticed.'

'Didn't Florence tell you what a sensitive guy I am?'

'I didn't notice. How insensitive of me.'

'Then she's losing her touch.'

'Maybe I just wasn't interested.'

'Good.'

'Good?' She opened her eye in surprise.

'Yes. Good. Too many single women have been interested in Florence's glowing descriptions of me. What she fails to tell them is that *I'm* not interested.'

'You're gay?' Laurel hoped her voice didn't betray the disappointment she couldn't stop from feeling.

He looked at her steadily, his grey eyes amused and challenging.

'Now, if you weren't so ... indisposed ... at the moment, I might be tempted to prove to you just how much I enjoy sex with women. But in the circumstances you'll just have to take my word for it.'

Laurel blinked, unprepared for his blatant sexual challenge. She remembered how her hormones had got the better of her when she'd first seen him, and she felt her body begin to respond.

'OK,' she squeaked. *Way to go, Laurel,* she thought as he gave her a knowing smile. *Why not be done with it and ask him to prove it anyway? Act like a complete idiot, why don't you?*

'Are you thirsty? You sound ...'

... Like a twit!

'Yes. Water. I'm very thirsty,'

She realised her mistake immediately. Instead of getting them off the disturbing topic of sex, it kept it firmly in her mind as he moved closer to help her. With a gentle arm around her shoulders, he helped her raise her head, and held a cup to her lips. Laurel forced herself to concentrate on not spilling the cool liquid, but was unable to stop the fine trembling his touch caused. She rarely let a man touch her. The doctor hadn't counted – he was doing his job and didn't regard her personally. But Daniel French

22

was a different matter. He was getting entirely too personal, and God help her, she was letting him. She couldn't even blame the accident, because he had gotten to her from the moment she'd set eyes on him.

She took a few sips, and then he laid her back down. She whispered her thanks, and sighed as he withdrew his touch and she relaxed against the pillows.

'Are you tired? Shall I leave you to sleep?'

'Probably.'

'You're probably tired, or I should probably leave?'

'Actually, *I* should probably leave. But I suppose we'll be charged for the whole night, and whatever stuff the doc gave me ... well, let's just say that for tonight I'm past caring.'

'You mustn't be in any hurry to leave, Laurel. The doctor said you need to rest, and you'll be in pain for a while. There's no rush.'

'Yes, there is. I've got to get back to work. I can't lay here like Lady Muck just because of a few bruises.' She'd managed before. She had no choice. If she didn't work she didn't eat. Plus they were unlikely to let her stay at the restaurant if she wasn't pulling her weight. She'd cope. She had to. No matter how tempting it might be to let Daniel French pick up the tab for a few more days' rest in these fresh, clean sheets instead of her ratty old sleeping bag.

'I doubt if you'll have any work to go back to for a while,' Daniel said. 'The lorry took out most of the frontage.'

But the impact of his statement was lost as she slipped into a healing sleep.

Daniel stayed where he sat on the edge of her bed, watching her slumber deepen. He ran a hand over his weary face. It had been a hell of a day. He'd never known such fear as when he saw Florence walk innocently into the path of the runaway lorry as it headed towards the restaurant. Despite being in her eighties, he had always regarded her as immortal. The prospect of her dying was anathema to him. He had never allowed himself to contemplate it. And the thought of losing her under those wheels …

But he hadn't lost Florence, and it was thanks to this girl who now lay battered and bruised in a hospital bed.

He reached out to stroke a finger down Laurel's clear, soft cheek, but stopped just short of touching her.

He stood abruptly, turning away. It was time to go. He'd done his duty. He'd promised Florence he'd stay until the girl regained consciousness and had assured her that the older woman was safe.

He reached the door and looked back. She was sleeping peacefully now. No reason for him to stay. But he didn't open it. Laurel Park bothered him, and he was reluctant to leave until he could put his finger on just what it was about her that was doing this. He leaned against the wall by the door, just as he had when the doctor had examined her earlier. Daniel Park wasn't a man used to having his equilibrium upset by any woman, especially not some stroppy little waitress he knew next to nothing about.

She was attractive enough under the bruises, if you liked petite, green-eyed blondes with a penchant for attempting to break men's fingers. He flexed his own digits, his smile reluctant. And she had guts. Not only had she stood up to him, but she'd risked her life to rescue her friend. She had clearly seen the danger, but she hadn't hesitated. He had wondered earlier whether she was trying to con the older woman. What Florence had told him about the mugging seemed to smack of a set-up. But her selfless act of bravery today, coupled with her genuine grief when she thought she'd failed, convinced him of her true fondness for Florence. And Florence was extremely fond of Laurel too.

She had been distraught over her young friend's

injuries, insisting on coming to the hospital, to the extent that he had been worried the stress of the situation would affect her own health. That's why he promised to stay and persuaded her to get some rest, arranging a room for her as well as getting the patient moved into a private room to reassure Florence that she was getting the best possible attention.

Laurel was stronger than she looked, and by some miracle the damage done to her wasn't as bad as he had expected. When he'd seen her flying through the air like a rag doll, he was sure she was dead. But the doctor had confirmed that apart from her wrist, there were no other broken bones. Her ribs were badly bruised, as was the side of her face; she had a number of superficial cuts, but nothing that should leave a scar. She should be back to normal in a week or two, although the plaster would be on her wrist for a bit longer.

So, everything was all right. Florence was safe. Laurel was on the mend. He rubbed his eyes. It was gone midnight. Time to go home. He'd leave a message for Florence with the staff, and return in the morning to pick her up.

Laurel sighed in her sleep, and Daniel moved close again to reassure himself that she was all right. He frowned when he remembered asking the restaurant staff about contacting Laurel's family. They said she didn't have any. Florence had insisted on taking on the role of next of kin when the ambulance staff had arrived. Laurel's fellow workers had been busy dealing with the aftermath of the accident and no one else had been free to do it. There had been a lot of shocked people needing reassurance and support, although miraculously no one else had been hurt. Just Laurel. And apparently she had no one.

Hell! What was wrong with him? Was he going soft?

He needed to get some sleep. For a fleeting moment he

had remembered what it had felt like, being young and alone. His parents had only been interested in scoring points off each other and using him as a weapon. When they'd both remarried, he'd found himself left at boarding school for the holidays because neither of them wanted to him around to spoil their newfound 'happiness' with their latest partners. But he'd had Florence to rescue him, and from that moment he'd never felt that soul-deep aloneness again. That Florence was the only person who had ever managed to touch him emotionally might concern his godmother, but it suited him just fine. He'd seen the destructive power of love time and again as his parents had both failed in their attempts to find the perfect partner. They'd each notched up three marriages and countless affairs before his father died of a heart attack and his mother had been killed in a car accident a few months later. Neither had found happiness. Daniel had decided long ago that he wouldn't go down that road. So why was he in the least bit concerned about Laurel Park being alone? She was better off that way. And so was he.

Daniel opened the door and slipped quietly out of the room without looking back.

'You've got to talk to her, Daniel,' Florence didn't bother with a greeting when he arrived the next day.

'Good morning to you too,' he responded, kissing her cheek. 'I assume you mean the patient is asserting her independence.'

'Have you seen her already? The silly girl thinks she can go home today and get back to work. You mustn't let her, Daniel.'

'I spoke to her last night. She's over eighteen, Florence. She's entitled to make her own decisions.' He'd decided after a restless night that it would be better to let Laurel Park go her own way if she really wanted to. She didn't want help and he certainly didn't want to get involved.

With Florence due to leave for Monaco, the situation could be neatly tied up within twenty-four hours.

He followed his godmother along the hall to Laurel's room. She was arguing with a nurse.

'Look, I know you're just doing your job, but I want to leave. I feel OK, and I need to get home.'

'Well, you don't look OK,' Florence declared. She turned to the nurse with a sweet smile. 'I wonder if you could leave us for a while please, nurse?'

The woman didn't need to be asked twice. Daniel took up his usual spot by the door and did his best to hide his smile. Watching Florence in action was always entertaining. Laurel wouldn't know what hit her.

'Is he on guard?' Laurel asked, deciding that attack was the best form of defence. She had to get out of here. She had to find out if she had a job – and a home, such as it was – to go back to. While she was glad to see that Florence was OK, she was in no mood to meekly sit here when she didn't know what had happened at the restaurant after the accident. Her friend Joanne was three months pregnant. No one seemed to know if she was all right. She didn't even know if Joanne and Chris knew where she was. What if Jo had been hurt too? What if worrying about what had happened to Laurel brought on a miscarriage? Those two were the closest she had to a family. Only they, and more recently Florence, knew or cared anything about her. She had to see them.

'Of course not, dear,' Florence soothed, ignoring her belligerent tone and taking a seat. 'He's just too much of a gentleman to sit down whilst ladies are standing. Why don't you sit down, then we can talk.'

'I haven't got time, Florence. I have to get back to the restaurant.'

'I understand your concern, dear, but there's no need.'

'But Joanne …'

'Is fine. I checked yesterday when we were waiting for

27

you to wake up. I told her you're going to be all right. But I'm afraid if she sees you in this state she'll think I was lying. Why don't you telephone her so that you can both be reassured?'

Laurel started to protest.

'She's right, you know. Your bruises are coming out and your face looks quite spectacular,' Daniel interrupted.

He looked annoyed. Oh heck! Why didn't he just take Florence and go away? She knew what she looked like – she'd had quite a fright when she'd staggered into the bathroom early this morning. That was another reason to worry – would the boss let her waitress looking like that? If not, she'd try and talk him into letting her do the paperwork – he was always moaning about having to do it. She planned on playing up the 'heroine' angle – he couldn't refuse her work when she'd got to look like this by saving one of his customers, could he? If he still didn't bite, she was in trouble because she couldn't peel vegetables or wash up with her wrist in plaster. She took a breath and her ribs protested.

'Thanks, just what a girl wants to hear – that's she's spectacular,' she mocked.

Daniel shook his head and sighed.

'Well, if you insist on leaving,' declared Florence, 'I shall put off my trip. You'll need a place to stay.'

'No!' she protested, at the same time that Daniel asked, 'Why?'

Laurel finally gave in and sat down. The painkillers she'd been given when she awoke this morning were wearing off. Everything throbbed and she could barely think straight. Daniel watched her, his narrowed gaze taking in the pallor not quite hidden by the multi-coloured bruises.

'You can't put off your trip,' Laurel protested. 'Your arthritis will get worse.'

'I doubt it will be any more uncomfortable than your

injuries, and as they're my fault, I'll cope for a while longer. The thing is, my dear,' Florence explained gently, 'the restaurant was a mess. The whole frontage was damaged. I doubt if it'll be open again for some time, and it won't be safe for you to stay there.'

'So I'll stay with Jo and Chris,' Laurel said, hiding her panic.

'No need. I'm taking you home with me. Monaco can wait for a week or two.'

Daniel stood away from the wall.

'Florence, your flight is booked for tomorrow,' he reminded her. 'Surely the sensible thing for Laurel to do is stay here a bit longer until she can make her own arrangements. There's no need for you to change your plans.'

Laurel felt trapped. She couldn't stay here. It was too expensive, and if what Florence said was true, she needed to get her stuff out of the restaurant building and find another job. She would have to sleep on the floor at Jo and Chris's for a couple of nights until she sorted something else. She almost groaned out load at the thought. She looked longingly at the fine cotton sheets she'd slept in last night, keeping her gaze away from Florence's sympathy and Daniel's irritation.

She didn't know why he was getting so stony-faced. She wanted to get out of here, and he wanted her gone. They were on the same side, for God's sake. So why did she feel as though he was about to explode? She couldn't help but feel disappointed, even as she told herself to stop being stupid. But last night ... maybe it was the drugs, or the shock, she didn't know ... she'd felt a connection. Today, the familiar feeling of being in the way was back.

'I agree, Daniel, darling, Laurel is in no fit state to leave hospital, let alone find somewhere else to live.'

'Somewhere to live?' he asked, frowning.

'Florence, I told you, I'll stay with Jo and Chris.'

'But ...' she began to protest.

Laurel smiled, willing her friend to give it up.

'I can't stay here. It'll be OK, I promise. You mustn't put off your holiday.'

Florence looked doubtful. 'Well, you must at least let us take you there. You don't even have your purse with you, child.'

'Good point,' she conceded, relieved. 'OK.'

It took a while for the discharge to be arranged, and a supply of painkillers to be dispensed. Florence and Daniel went to arrange it, leaving her alone.

Laurel was almost finished dressing when Daniel came back into the room. He spotted her through the open bathroom door. She had pulled her injured wrist out of its sling and was struggling to button her blouse.

'Here, let me help.'

Daniel didn't give her the chance to argue as he took over the task, his cool fingers brushing gently against her sensitive skin as he fastened the remaining buttons.

'OK?' he asked softly.

Laurel swallowed hard, feeling her skin flush with mortification. She didn't know what was worse – the physical pain of trying to dress herself, or the mental pain of submitting to the tempting, delicious torture of feeling Daniel French's hands on her body. She hadn't been up to getting her bra on, and she felt sure he must notice her nipples standing proud through the thin material. And it got worse.

'Actually,' she admitted reluctantly. 'I, er ... couldn't do my skirt up.'

Daniel took a deep breath. 'OK, where?'

Miserably, she lifted her chin, and indicated over her shoulder with her good hand to the opening at the back of her skirt.

He moved around behind her and lifted her blouse to expose the open zip. He took his time pulling it up and fastening the button at her waist before smoothing the cotton material back over her skirt. Laurel stood frozen, watching him in the mirror.

He looked up, catching her.

'Anything else?'

Laurel licked dry lips and shook her head, all the time held by his steady gaze. He focussed on her mouth, and for a moment his cool grey eyes blazed hot.

'No,' she said, both answering him and denying her reaction to that look. 'Thanks. I'm ready to go now.'

Daniel blinked, and the coolness returned.

'Fine. Let's go. Florence is waiting.'

'You mustn't let her put off her trip,' she insisted. 'I'll be OK.'

Daniel said nothing for a moment, then he nodded.

'I'll drop her off first, and then take you wherever you want to go.'

As she followed him slowly out of the room, Laurel felt like a fool. What was she thinking? Perhaps it was the whack on her head that was making her imagine lust in Daniel's eyes just now. No man in his right mind would fancy her at the moment – she looked like she'd done a few rounds with a prize fighter. Just because his touch had awoken her deeply buried libido, there was no chance of him wanting to do anything about it. He couldn't wait to get shot of her. And that was just how Laurel wanted it. Wasn't it?

Chapter Three

Daniel stood in the doorway of the restaurant storeroom grim-faced, his fists clenched at his sides.

Laurel's friend Chris stood silently watching him.

'*This* is where she lives?' Daniel asked in disbelief, surveying the windowless room with floor to ceiling shelving around its bare grey walls. The floor was covered with worn, cracked tiles. The shelves were stacked with catering supplies, except for a small corner which had been cleared. There, Laurel kept her worldly goods – a sleeping bag and pillow that looked like they'd seen better days, a rucksack, and a couple of boxes, one stacked with neatly folded clothes, the other with books.

'Yeah. Home sweet home. Beats the streets.'

Daniel shook his head, his mind trying to come to terms with what his eyes were showing him.

'Why the hell doesn't she find herself a decent place? She's working, earning.'

Chris surveyed Daniel's expensive leather jacket, his expression belligerent.

'The pay's barely enough to cover a decent meal in this place. There's nothing round here she could rent. If she moved out to where she could afford, it would be too far to commute to work. And round those places the pay's even worse than here.'

'So why the hell doesn't she get a better job?' Daniel could feel his disbelief give way to frustration. 'She's qualified, isn't she?'

Chris laughed. 'Yeah. Four A-levels. She worked herself into the ground to get 'em and support herself at the same time. But if you want get out of the gutter you need a degree these days, mate. All she can find is more of the same. Firms looking for trainees either take 'em at eighteen, or when they leave uni. Most of 'em won't even give her an interview. Too busy looking after their own.' He muttered the last, but Daniel heard and understood the belligerent dig at the 'them and us' society.

Daniel eyed the young man, annoyed by his attitude. This morning was not going according to plan. He'd expected to take Laurel to her friends and walk away. But she'd insisted that she needed to collect her 'stuff' from the restaurant. He thought she'd meant her coat and purse, not everything she owned. Only when she had seen for herself that it had been boarded up and locked solid did she agree to let Daniel take her across town to where this lad and his girlfriend Joanne shared a grotty bedsit. By then she'd been exhausted and in no fit state to argue when Chris, who had a key, had offered to come back with Daniel to get whatever she wanted from their mutual workplace.

His girlfriend had been fussing over Laurel as they'd left, and Daniel had soon realised that the pair had seen him as the solution to Laurel's problems. Chris had spent the journey explaining that their boss had stayed long enough to clear the till and board the place up before leaving for his bar in Spain. Without adequate insurance and with a mountain of debts, he had preferred to walk away than attempt to claim against the driver's insurance and reopen what had been a struggling business. Laurel and her friends were unemployed, and Laurel was homeless. Injured and homeless.

Daniel took a deep breath. God, what a mess! He was just glad that Florence hadn't insisted she come with them. She had started to argue when he dropped her off first, but in the end she too had been worn out by the trauma of the accident and had agreed to trust him to see Laurel safely to her friends. He frowned. Maybe she'd agreed a little too quickly after all. He was beginning to think the whole world was conspiring against him where Laurel Park was concerned. If Florence knew the girl and her situation as well as she claimed, she would have known what he'd discover – that Laurel's friends had no room for her and that it was impossible for her to return to the restaurant. He wouldn't put it past the old girl to have set this whole thing up. She knew that he didn't want to get involved. But she'd also known that he'd not be able to walk away when he saw the reality of Laurel's situation, damn her!

'Help me get this lot into my car,' he said, keeping his temper to himself.

'What about Laurel? Will you help her?' Chris asked as he grabbed the rucksack and sleeping bag.

'Do I have a choice?' he bit out, hefting the box of books.

Chris raised both hands. 'Don't take it out on me, man. I'd help her if I could. She's been a good friend to me and Jo. But the only place we've got for her is our floor, and she can't sleep there in her state.'

'You wouldn't consider giving up your side of the bed for her then?'

Daniel's sarcasm went straight over his head.

'I would. Yeah, I would. But Laurel won't have it. Proud, she is. She'd see through all of us – even the old lady. That's why you've got to be smart. She won't take no hand-outs.'

So Florence had been involved. He might have guessed.

'What makes you think she won't see through me?'

Chris grinned.

'She will. But I reckon you're the sort of guy who'll win anyway.'

Daniel ran an agitated hand through his hair. It was obvious that Laurel's little gang – his own godmother included – had decided that he should be her knight in shining armour. But this particular damsel in distress had more in common with the dragon, and wouldn't take kindly to being rescued, however close to complete disaster she was. The worst of it was, he knew that they were right. He was big enough and bloody-minded enough to take her on and win. He might even enjoy it. He could sort proud little Miss Laurel Park out – find her a job, a home, even some decent clothes to cover that delectable little body of hers – and not even care about what had put that tree-sized chip on her shoulder.

But then he remembered the feel of her soft skin against the back of his hands as he'd fastened her clothes in the hospital and of her surprisingly curvy hips under his palm as he'd smoothed her blouse down over her skirt. He saw again in his mind's eye her stoicism as she endured the pain of her injuries, and her grief when she thought that she'd failed to save Florence.

And he wondered if this just might be a battle for which the price of victory would be his own peace of mind.

Laurel was dreading their return. It hadn't taken her long to realise that she couldn't impose herself on Jo and Chris. No way would she let Chris give up his half of the bed for her as Jo had suggested. With Jo expecting, it was important that he get out and find work as soon as possible and if he couldn't get a decent night's sleep he wouldn't stand a chance. Nor did she want to get in the way of the couple as they prepared for the birth of their baby. And much as she loved them both, she couldn't stomach hanging around when they got all lovey-dovey – which they did with nauseating frequency these days.

Laurel felt defeated as her mind searched frantically for a solution. But short of stealing Chris's key and sneaking back to the restaurant, she had few options. She had a few pounds in her purse, but not enough for a hotel. She had a bit saved, but it wouldn't last long. There might be a hostel bed available, but the last time she'd resorted to that she'd been robbed – and she'd been able-bodied then. In her present state she was a sitting duck. The council housing department wouldn't be open on a Sunday. Not that she expected much from them.

If she went to Florence, she would put off her trip, and Laurel didn't want her to do that, especially after the fright she'd had. No, the old lady needed to get away to the sun where she could relax. This meant that Laurel needed yet another favour from Daniel French. She had no choice.

She barely had time to accept the thought when he walked into the bedsit, filling the tiny space with his vibrant maleness. He looked grim, although he was gentle and polite with Jo. Laurel stayed where she was, propped up on the bed, hardly able to look at him when he sat on the edge of it to talk to her.

'How are you feeling?'

'OK. Did you get my stuff?'

'It's in the car.'

Laurel looked down at her hands, knowing she had to ask, but reluctant. He hadn't actually offered to put her up, only to pay for her to stay at the hospital. What if he said no? What if he said yes? Laurel hated to ask anyone for anything, and this man was a stranger to her – a stranger who stirred unknown and unwelcome feelings in her. Just feeling the mattress sag as he sat on it had sent her pulse racing. Her overactive imagination pictured him leaning closer, stroking her cheek as she offered her lips for his kiss. Some of what she was feeling blossomed into a rosy blush on her pale cheeks.

When Daniel actually did lean closer in concern for her sudden hectic colour, Laurel flinched back. His cold-eyed withdrawal left her burning with shame.

For the first time in a long time, Laurel admitted to herself that she was scared. Her life hadn't been great, but for the past few years she'd at least been in control. Suddenly, her shaky foundations had collapsed, leaving her lost and vulnerable.

'Are you ready to go?'

Her head shot up as she gazed at him in shock. She hadn't asked. She'd said she'd be staying here. It was obvious that her instinctive reaction to his nearness had offended him. So what on earth was he saying?

Daniel returned her uncertain look with cool determination.

'Your friends clearly haven't got the space for you. You don't have enough money in your purse to pay for a hotel ...'

'You looked in my purse?' she gasped, outraged.

'That was me,' confessed Chris. 'The boss left some cash for you before he hopped it. I put it in your purse. It's not much, Laurel. The bastard took most of the takings.'

'I, on the other hand, have a large house and a debt to repay.'

'You don't ...'

'Owe you? Yes I do, Laurel. You saved the life of the one person who means anything to me. So however much you hate me, or the idea of staying under my roof, it's tough. You're out of options, and you're coming home with me.'

'I don't hate you,' she denied automatically.

Daniel gave a crooked smile. 'Well, that's a start. Perhaps I can expect some polite conversation at least.'

'But ...'

'No buts. I'm offering you room and board for as long as you need it.'

'I'll go to the council offices tomorrow. And the job agencies. I won't stay for long,' she insisted.

Daniel shrugged. 'Fair enough.'

Laurel looked at him with suspicion. 'I mean it.'

'I have no doubt you do. So, are you ready to go?'

She fought a brief internal battle as she reminded herself of all the times she had been forced to take people's reluctant charity, while her heart was doing somersaults at the thought of spending more time with this man. She'd never met anyone like Daniel French before, never been affected by any man until now. If she had any other choice at this moment, she would grab it. But a choice was something she didn't have.

It seemed ironic that, when she'd been growing up she'd dreamt of some handsome prince riding into her life to rescue her. Now, even as she felt her pulse race at the thought of spending more time with this modern-day version of a knight in shining armour, she hated that she needed his help.

With a sigh, she nodded, resenting the look of satisfaction on his handsome face.

Laurel had once worked as a cleaner in a house like Daniel's. Never in a million years had she expected to find herself a guest in one. The elegant Georgian townhouse was situated in a quiet square complete with its own oasis of greenery in the centre. Only residents were meant to enjoy the small park, however, as it was protected by high railings and a locked gate. She smiled grimly as she remembered the night she'd sneaked into a similar place and slept under a bush. *What goes around comes around*, she thought. She wondered what Daniel would think if he knew everything. Maybe she should tell him. It would help maintain the distance between them if he knew just how far below him on the social scale Laurel came. *Mind you*, she thought bitterly, *he knew enough already*. Florence, in her well-meaning but infuriating way, had seen to that.

'How far are we from a bus stop?' she asked as he opened the front door and gestured her in.

'I have no idea,' he responded, blank faced.

Laurel rolled her eyes. 'Too posh for public transport?'

Daniel's eyes narrowed. Laurel sighed. 'OK, that was uncalled for. I'm sorry. Really. I just ...'

'Shut up, Laurel, before you dig yourself an even deeper hole.'

She was relieved to see the amusement back in his expression. If she was going to have to stay here, she'd better stop having a go at him. It wasn't his fault that she found him and everything to do with him so overwhelming. It was her natural defence system to come out fighting, but perhaps that wasn't appropriate in the circumstances.

'OK, sorry.'

A raised eyebrow was his only reaction to her reluctant apology, before he led her into the house.

If she hadn't been worn out and sore, she might have appreciated the light-filled hall, the high ceilings, and the serenity of the place. But right now Laurel was having trouble putting one foot in front of the other. She followed him obediently towards the back of the house and into a beautifully appointed kitchen.

'Take a seat.' He gestured towards the scrubbed pine table over in the bay window overlooking the garden. 'I'll make us something to eat.'

'You cook?' she was surprised into asking.

He smiled, yet Laurel got the impression he wasn't amused.

'Like anyone else who lives alone, I had to learn how to feed myself or starve.'

Laurel flushed. 'Not necessarily. I know people who live on takeaways and sandwiches.'

'Well, I have a bit more respect for my body than that.' He gave her a narrow eyed stare as she stood uncertainly in the doorway. 'You'd better sit down before you fall down. Don't worry, I won't poison you.'

She moved slowly, her energy almost depleted, and sank into the chair he held out for her with a grateful sigh.

'Thanks.'

'You're welcome.'

Laurel had to bite her tongue to stop her instinctive 'yeah right' response. She was stuck here for a day or two. She was too weak to fight right now, and anyway, it wasn't his fault. It hadn't been difficult to see that they'd both been manipulated, first by Florence, then Chris and Jo.

'I'm really sorry about this,' she began, but he glanced at his watch and cut her off.

'I'm sure. Let's leave this conversation until you've got some food in you and had some rest. I also want to go over and check on Florence and make sure she's got a lift to the airport tomorrow. I'm in back to back meetings most of the week, otherwise I'd do it myself.'

He moved across to the large stainless steel refrigerator and examined its contents. Laurel couldn't help but notice what a lovely backside he had as he reached inside.

'Omelettes, I think. With cheese and mushrooms?'

She blinked as he turned to catch her ogling his rear end.

'Er, actually, I'm not very hungry.'

He straightened, depositing a carton of eggs and various packets on the island worktop separating the main part of the kitchen with the breakfast area where she sat.

'But I am. And you haven't eaten for at least twenty-four hours. If you want to get back to work, you're going to need to eat.'

She bristled. She knew that. But she'd gone a lot longer than a day without food before and survived. But sucking in a deep breath spoiled her indignation as pain engulfed her.

'Oh sheesh! I'm going to have to stop doing that!' she gasped, leaning back and putting her good arm to her chest.

'What?'

'Breathing. Bloody painful.' She closed her eyes and waited for the agony to recede.

When she opened her eyes Daniel was standing over her.

'You're in no fit state to be out of hospital,' he grated.

She just about stopped herself from flinching away from his angry tone.

'You said yourself I'm not dying. I just need rest.'

He looked as though he was going to argue, but Laurel kept her gaze steady, refusing to be intimidated. After long moments he gave a brief nod and moved back to the counter.

'You're right. I'll show you to your room in a minute. But first you eat.'

'OK,' she conceded, glad that a row had been averted. 'But no mushrooms.'

The food was delicious, but Laurel struggled to eat it. She didn't know whether it was her physical discomfort or the disturbing proximity of Daniel French, but her appetite really was non-existent. She was aware of his gaze as she forced herself to begin eating the fluffy omelette he'd placed in front of her, rich with cheese and ham.

She ate slowly, trying not to look at him. It was hard to resist, but she stopped herself from meeting his gaze. Instead, she found herself watching him through lowered lashes. She was mesmerised by his firm lips and chiselled jaw moving as he chewed, and his throat as he swallowed. She found herself swallowing her own food at the same time, as though her body was trying to synchronise with his. When his tongue emerged to lick his lips, Laurel knew that enough was enough. She carefully placed her fork on the plate and sat back.

'Finished?' He asked, his voice strained.

One quick glance confirmed her suspicions. He knew she'd been watching him. His gaze was full of the knowledge, and he didn't look happy about it. Of course he knew. She felt foolish and embarrassed. He probably had women falling over themselves to share a meal – to share anything – with him. Daniel French was a seriously sexy man. But that didn't mean she should repay his hospitality by embarrassing him or herself. No. What she needed to do was get some rest and get out of his orbit as quickly as possible.

'It ... it was lovely,' she replied, her tight throat making her voice husky. 'But I really am tired. Would ... would you mind if I just go to bed?'

'Of course not. I'll show you upstairs. Leave that,' he commanded when she picked up her plate. 'I'll load the dishwasher later.'

'I'm capable of clearing up after myself,' she retorted.

'And you're capable of collapsing if you don't get some rest soon. For God's sake, woman, just stop arguing and come with me.'

With a sigh, Laurel followed him. This was not going well. She climbed the stairs slowly, refusing to look up at his delicious rear as he ascended ahead of her. Half way up she stopped to catch her breath, and Daniel was at her side in a moment.

'Do you want me to carry you?' he asked.

She raised a hand as if to ward him off.

'Don't you dare!'

She looked at his frosty expression, and gave him a sheepish smile. 'Look, I don't mean to be rude, but if you pick me up I'm likely to scream the place down. The less contact these ribs have with anything, the better.'

'Good point,' he responded grimly. 'If you're sure you can manage, I'll go ahead and turn the bed down.'

'Yeah. Thanks. I'll be OK. Sorry to be such a pest.'

Laurel could have sworn his expression softened briefly before he remembered himself and turned away. With a wistful sigh, she put her good hand on the smooth bannister and began to follow him.

When Daniel returned home later that evening, he expected to find Laurel asleep in the guest bedroom he'd shown her to. But when he quietly opened the door to check that she was all right, the rumpled bed was empty, as was the en-suite bathroom.

At first he thought that she had left, but then he remembered that he still had all but her rucksack in the boot of his car. After all the fuss she'd made about her meagre worldly goods, he couldn't believe she would leave without them.

His search for her ended in his study, where he found her, in a pool of light from a standard lamp sitting in a large leather wing-backed chair, fast asleep. Her bare feet were propped up on a matching footstool, her head rested against the high back of the armchair. Her face was turned to one side, concealing her black eye and bruises from his gaze. Her blonde hair was loose, surrounding her pale face and falling across her shoulders. On her lap a book lay open.

Unwilling to wake her, Daniel sat down in the matching armchair and watched her sleep. She really was an exquisite creature. His fingers itched to reach out and see if her hair was as soft as it looked. He already knew how perfect her skin felt.

She'd obviously managed to get herself undressed and to pull on a T-shirt and a pair of joggers, and she'd left the sling off of her plastered wrist. Instead, it rested against the arm of the chair, its bulky presence reminding him of the appalling fear he'd felt when she'd been hit by the runaway lorry as it ploughed into the restaurant.

Daniel marvelled at how one's orderly life could change so dramatically in the space of a few hours. He'd gone out for a simple meal with his godmother yesterday, expecting to wish her a good holiday and return home to get on with some paperwork. Twenty-four hours later, he'd found himself promising Florence that he would take responsibility for her young friend and make sure that she stayed with him until she was completely recovered. He knew that Laurel would fight him tooth and nail. The woman had a seriously large chip on her shoulder. They'd have to sort that out. Whatever wrongs she perceived had been done against her were none of his doing. Laurel Park needed to learn not to punish every man for the sins of a few. Given her ethereal beauty, he had no doubt that men had tried to take advantage. Hell, he was tempted himself, even when she was battered and bruised! But he'd given Florence his word to protect her. Much as he'd enjoy exploring the attraction that flared between them, he now felt duty bound to keep his hands to himself. He could hardly take her to his bed and then tell his godmother that he'd acted in the girl's best interests. There could be no future or any sort of relationship between them – just sex. He didn't do commitment. He'd seen what it did to his parents. And despite her bravado, Laurel Park would be vulnerable. She would expect more from him than he was prepared to give.

He couldn't help his body's involuntary reaction to the image of the sleeping woman in front of him, however. Whatever his mind had decided, his hormones were urging him to touch her, to take the tantalising electricity between them to its obvious conclusion – in his bed.

Laurel sighed and rolled her head from one side to the other, exposing her bruised and swollen flesh. Daniel felt his arousal subside as guilt rose.

She was injured, in pain, and he was weaving sexual fantasies around her. What sort of a man was he? She had no job, no home, and no money. Even he wasn't such an unfeeling bastard as to take advantage of her, was he?

It took him a few moments to realise that she was awake. She'd turned her head again just enough to allow her to regard him steadily through her good eye. Daniel leant forward, resting his forearms on his thighs, not trusting his wayward body to behave.

'How do you feel?'

'OK. I needed to sit up. I couldn't sleep lying down.'

'I'll get you some more pillows. You can't sleep down here all night.'

'Thanks. Did you see Florence?'

Daniel smiled. 'Yes. She's all packed and raring to go. I just hope I've got that amount of energy when I'm her age.'

'She's amazing, isn't she? I've never known anyone like her.'

'Well, thanks to you, she's looking forward to a well-deserved holiday instead of …'

'Don't, please,' she shuddered. 'She's OK. So am I, even if I don't look it.' She chuckled as she watched him open his mouth and close it again. 'It's all right. I wasn't fishing for compliments. I looked in the mirror. What a sight! I'll be frightening children and animals for a few days, that's for sure.'

'Well, you don't have to worry about that. No children or animals here.'

'No. I noticed. This is a big house for one person. It must be lonely.'

Daniel felt a wave of disappointment hit. He'd heard that line so many times, usually accompanied by a woman's offer to stay and keep him company. The trouble was, he knew that they were more interested in his wealth and status than truly easing his loneliness. And now Laurel Park was playing true to her gender's form and applying for the role of house pet to a rich man. He'd thought better of her.

'It suits my needs,' he said, his tone clipped. 'I prefer living alone.'

Laurel's face took on a guarded expression. Daniel wondered if the twinge of discomfort he felt might be regret. Maybe he shouldn't have been so sharp, but it had needed to be said. He didn't want her getting any stupid ideas.

'I can relate to that,' she said quietly, surprising him again. 'I've spent my life trying to find some space of my own.'

'So how did you end up living in a restaurant stockroom?'

She shrugged. 'It was only supposed to be temporary while I looked for a better job.' She sighed. 'It's taken longer than I expected, mainly because I liked working at the restaurant. But I'll have to get on with it now and find something with more security.'

'Why don't you just go home?'

She stiffened slightly, her gaze wary.

'What do you mean?'

'To your family,' he replied, becoming impatient. 'Surely they didn't approve of you living in a storeroom. Shouldn't you at least let them know about the accident?'

Laurel studied him in disbelief. She was sure that Florence had told him. Hadn't she been asking him to give Laurel a job when she'd interrupted them in the restaurant? She shook her head in confusion. No, Florence had apologised, she'd looked guilty. So why was Daniel acting as though a simple phone call to some alleged family would solve her problems and get her out of his hair?

For a moment she was distracted by his hair. It was so dark, making her own blonde locks seem even paler. So beautifully cut, framing his strong face and hugging his tanned neck. Laurel itched to reach out and run her fingers up his nape and onto his scalp. Would his hair be as soft as it looked, or hard, like his expression?

'Well?' he asked.

She blinked, feeling hot colour flood her face as her gaze met his.

'W-what?'

'Your family. Where are they?'

'God knows,' she responded instinctively.

Daniel sighed and raked an agitated hand through his hair. Laurel swallowed hard. That's exactly where she'd wanted to touch him.

'When did you last see any of them?' he demanded.

She couldn't help it. She laughed. Either he really didn't have a clue, or he thought she'd lied to Florence and was demanding the truth from her own lips. Well, if that's what he wanted …

'When I was dumped under a laurel bush in a park a couple of hours after I was born,' she told him, keeping her voice light and mocking, just as she'd learned to do. No one would ever know how hard she had worked to perfect her delivery of that damning phrase; how hard she'd fought against the hurt and shame of knowing that her mother had given her life and then thrown her away. 'Where else would I get a stupid name like "Laurel"? It's just as well I wasn't found under a privet hedge. And it's lucky I was a girl. What on earth would they have called a boy? Shrub? Or maybe they'd have named me after the dog who found me – his name was Rex, I think.'

'Laurel Park.' Daniel breathed her name, shock robbing his voice of strength. He was silent for a long moment. 'You were found in a park?' he asked, his disgust obvious.

She nodded.

'Do you have any idea who you really are?' he asked softly.

She lifted her chin, her good eye blazing as she sat straighter. She ignored the pain which sliced across her chest.

'I'm Laurel Park, that's who I *really* am. I'm my own person, and it doesn't matter who gave me life. I've made it my own. That's what's important. '

Please don't pity me, she wanted to beg. *Don't look at me and see the discarded child! See me – Laurel! The*

48

person I am, in spite of it all!

She felt cold as she searched his carefully blank expression, watching for any clue to what he was thinking. Her heart pumped adrenaline through her body, blotting out the physical pain as she braced herself to flee. She'd spend her first sixteen years being regarded with pity and scorn for something she'd had no control over. When she'd finally escaped the care system, the indifferent foster homes, the pitying do-gooders, she'd vowed that she'd never, ever, let anyone use her background as an excuse to turn her back into a charity case. She'd succeed on her own. She didn't need anyone.

Yet here she was. Jobless, homeless, virtually penniless, and at the mercy of Daniel French. She cursed herself for telling him. What had she been thinking? She was so stupid. She could have played along with him and made a fake call and been out of here with her pride intact before he realised. But she'd been so sure he knew already and was playing some cruel game that she'd been caught off guard.

'Laurel, I ...'

'Don't!' She held up her good hand to stop him. 'Don't apologise for something that's not your fault. I won't. You asked and I told you. That's the end of it. It happened a long time ago and has nothing to do with now. Just forget I told you, OK?'

'I'm hardly going to do that,' he frowned. 'I accept that you've made a life for yourself, but frankly, it's not much of one right now, is it?'

Laurel wanted to slap him. That it was true didn't make his words less cruel.

'Well, I may not be some hot-shot investor with a posh house and a few mill in the bank, but hey! We can't all be perfect, can we?' she mocked.

Daniel regarded her steadily, his eyes and voice cool. 'No.'

He got up and walked over to the window. Laurel stared at his ramrod-stiff back, regretting that she'd angered him. She wished she'd met this man in another life. One where they were equals, free of baggage and suspicion, able to love each other ... *Whoa! Where had that come from? What was wrong with her, what was she thinking? Love? No way.* She swung her feet onto the floor and started to rise. She had to get out of here. Thinking about him like that was crazy, it was stupid, and it was dangerous.

'Where are you going?' He'd turned and was watching her.

'I'm tired. I'll go back upstairs.'

He nodded, but said nothing. He was probably glad to see the back of her. But as she turned to go, Laurel realised that she couldn't leave things like this.

'Daniel.'

He raised his eyebrows, waiting.

'I ... I'm sorry. That was a cheap shot. You've been kind, and I appreciate being allowed to stay here.'

He blew out an irritated breath. 'When are you going to stop using that chip on your shoulder like a weapon, Laurel? It's not a case of you being "allowed" − it's the least I can do − call it payment for services rendered if you like. But for God's sake, stop acting like you're some sort of pariah who doesn't deserve to be treated with consideration!'

She stared at him, speechless.

'You're welcome here, Laurel Park, because you saved my godmother's life. I'm concerned about your future for the same reason, OK?'

She nodded, using a shaking hand to brush her fine hair away from her hot face.

'OK,' she murmured. 'I'm s ...'

'Don't! Don't apologise for something that's not your fault, and I won't.'

She gave him a small, reluctant smile as her own words came back at her.

'OK.'

He nodded, his mouth softening from its grim angry line.

'Good. Now, you head up and I'll find those extra pillows.'

If Laurel had been capable, she'd have run from his disturbing presence. Instead, she made her slow and painful way back to her room. By the time she'd used the en-suite bathroom, Daniel had delivered two plump feather pillows and disappeared. As she lay propped against them, she could have sworn she could smell the essence of Daniel French on the fine Egyptian cotton.

'It's probably just his washing powder,' she whispered to herself, unwilling to admit that he was filling her senses, and in danger of becoming important to her.

Chapter Four

With the help of some painkillers, Laurel slept the clock round and woke to find the midday sun streaming through her window. For a while she lay still, savouring the luxury of fine sheets and sleeping in a real bed, letting herself dream for a moment that this was where she belonged.

But soon her practical mind took over, scorning her fanciful yearnings and reminding her that she needed to move on. She had no intention of outstaying her welcome. With a sigh she began to move, only to be reminded painfully of her injuries as her body protested. She groaned and fell back against the pillows, winded. Perhaps she should stay in bed? She was tempted, but didn't want to give in. She wondered where Daniel was. Not that she would ask him for help, but … it disturbed Laurel to realise that she wanted to see him. In the forty-eight hours since they'd first met, she had run the gamut of emotions with this man – lust, anger, grief, shame, and even gratitude. He'd taken over her life, and that frightened her, brought out her fighting instincts. She'd never met a man like him, and she doubted she'd meet another. And while part of her wanted to run as far and as fast as she could away from him, another part remembered that first sight of him in the restaurant and needed to stay and work out what it was about him that was different.

When she eventually made it to the kitchen she was exhausted. The simple acts of washing and dressing, and coming downstairs had taken a monumental effort. She sank into a chair and faced the fact that she was going nowhere today. She rested her head on her good hand as she glared at the bulky plaster on her other wrist and wondered why she wasn't so bothered about the prospect of staying in Daniel French's house for a little while longer.

Well, at least she could have a go at making a cup of tea for herself. Daniel had obviously gone to work. She remembered he'd said something about back to back meetings, so she presumed she had the place to herself for the rest of the day.

Propped against the kettle was a note.

Eat, sleep, relax. Use the phone if you need to, but stay at home or you'll frighten children and animals. D

Her ribs protested when she laughed and she had to sit down again until the pain passed.

She didn't feel much like eating, but she forced herself to have a bowl of soup. She was pathetically grateful that Daniel's kitchen boasted an electric tin opener, as her wrist was throbbing. Her painkillers were by her bed, and she put off going back for them, reasoning that if she went up she'd be unlikely to be fit to come down again any time soon. Instead, she rinsed her bowl single-handed and left it to drain and went in search of a telephone.

She had just pushed open the door of the study that she'd found sanctuary in last night when the phone on the desk began to ring. The sound startled her and she jumped, gasping in pain at the sudden movement. By the time she'd caught her breath, Daniel's answerphone had kicked in. Laurel hovered by the desk, listening to his deep velvet voice. She hoped that it would be him calling between meetings to see how she was, and was prepared to pick up the phone when the message ended if that proved to be the case. What she didn't expect was to hear the soft, petulant tones of a woman.

'Daniel, darling, where are you? I've been trying to reach you all weekend! Your mobile must be switched off. Didn't you get my messages? I thought I was going to see you at the Bellamy's on Saturday night. Daddy and I were so disappointed. I tried to call you at your office just now, but your PA is doing her usual Rottweiler act and wouldn't put me through. She said you couldn't be disturbed. You really must do something about her attitude. I need to talk to you. Darling Daniel, don't be cruel to me, please! Call me. As soon as you get this.'

Laurel slumped against the desk, feeling oddly let down. So Daniel French had a girlfriend. And a very unhappy one, by the sound of it. One who was feeling neglected because Daniel had spent the weekend sorting out Laurel's problems.

He'd never mentioned a girlfriend. Only that he lived alone. But it must be fairly serious judging by Daddy's disappointment at his no-show on Saturday. Perhaps that's why Daniel had been so impatient with her. While she'd been being difficult, he was contemplating his future father-in-law's annoyance.

Frowning, she wondered why he hadn't rung the woman and explained. Something didn't make sense. Even on a short acquaintance, she felt sure he'd have called if he'd had to break a date, instead of leaving her hanging like that. She was disappointed to think that Daniel French was the type to 'treat 'em mean to keep 'em keen'. Perhaps it was Florence's influence, but she'd thought he would be more considerate of people. He'd even been kind to her in his own gruff way.

She blew out an impatient breath, reaching for the phone. It was none of her business how he conducted his affairs. She should be thanking her lucky stars that he was some other woman's problem, and not hers. That she didn't like that idea one little bit was something she didn't want to consider.

After a fruitless couple of hours she returned to the leather armchair by the window bay and picked up the book she'd started the night before. But her head was spinning with the frustrations of the day and she gave up. Instead she gazed out at the garden, rich in late autumn colour. When she'd first seen it she'd felt such peace, as though she'd come home. She sat there, drinking it all in. Daniel's home was her idea of heaven. This room in particular had drawn her in. The book-lined shelves, antique walnut desk, and man-sized leather armchairs welcomed her. The rich colours of the rugs and cushions made it feel warm and cosy, and French windows framed the view of the lush garden, hidden from the outside world by high brick walls.

She could imagine how it would look out there in all the different seasons. In her mind's eye she could see the fresh green buds of new growth in the spring, the heady scent of roses in summer, and how it would sparkle with the stark, frosty beauty of winter. She wondered if Daniel looked after it himself, and if he enjoyed the sight of it as much as she did.

It would be so easy to give in to weakness and stay here for as long as Daniel would tolerate her. But she couldn't. He might say she was welcome, but she knew better. She'd been expected to feel 'welcome' in too many strangers' homes during her years in care, and she never had. She'd felt in the way, a nuisance; had even been told that by one or two. Some had tried harder than others, but no one else's house had ever felt like home to Laurel. The fact that this house did made it all the more important to leave quickly. It would never be her home, so there was no point in getting attached to it, or its sexy owner.

She'd stay for as long as it took the bruises to fade, she decided, and then she'd be off. Daniel's honour would have been satisfied, and what Florence didn't know couldn't worry her.

The fact that Daniel had a girlfriend made it even clearer to Laurel that she didn't belong here. So it was a good thing that, even if she couldn't summon the strength to go out to work right now, she had at least started laying some ground work by ringing a few agencies.

When Daniel let himself into the house that evening he found Laurel in the same place she had been the night before, absorbed in the book that had lain on her lap then. By the look of it, she'd read about half the story.

'You're a fast reader,' he commented, startling her.

The unguarded look of pleasure on her face when she registered his presence lasted a mere heartbeat before it was replaced by wary politeness.

'Hi. I hope you don't mind.' She gestured with the book. 'It's one of my favourites, so I couldn't resist.'

'No problem. It's no good to anyone stuck on a shelf unread.'

Laurel's smile lit up her face. 'Exactly. It's such a waste.'

'You like reading,' he said unnecessarily. *Hell! This girl short-circuited his brain when she smiled like that.* He turned away and placed his leather briefcase on the desk.

'Best entertainment on earth,' she agreed. 'With a book you can go anywhere, be anyone, do anything.'

'The ultimate escape?'

'Oh yeah. You wouldn't believe the places I've been and the things I've seen when I escape into one of these sweet babies. I can put up with anything in real life so long as I've got a good book to escape into.'

He sat down in the chair opposite her, enjoying her passionate advocacy of the written word.

'Why do you need a book? Surely if you've got a good imagination you can create your own escape in your own mind.'

'Of course you can. But there's just something about seeing into someone else's imagination, being able to share their vision and make it your own. I wouldn't have known about any of their worlds if I didn't have their words to show me. I'd have been stuck within the limits of my own experience, and that's exactly what I want to escape from.'

Daniel watched her smooth a hand over the pages in front of her. She really meant it. Yet she wasn't being self-pitying. She was simply explaining the joy she found in books. And having seen where she'd been living, and heard about her abandonment as a baby, he could understand why she wanted to forget her own reality for a while. He wondered about her life in the intervening years. It surprised him that he was even interested. He had nothing in common with Laurel Park, other than their mutual affection for Florence and beyond that he had no desire to go. While she might be tunnelling deep into his psyche to unearth a surprised admiration for her courage and determination, his cynical heart refused to believe she could be as untouched by the need to take advantage of people's goodwill as she appeared. In his experience women were naturally mercenary. Even Florence was an expert in getting her own way.

He was waiting for Laurel to fall from the pedestal on which Florence's accident had placed her. In fact, he would welcome it. She would be less of a problem to him if she played true to type instead of confounding him with her stubborn pride at every turn.

'Why didn't you take the book Florence wanted to give you?'

'You know why,' she said quietly.

'No. Tell me.'

She sighed and shifted in her seat, wincing in discomfort. 'It would have been stupid and irresponsible. It would've been ruined or nicked in record time. I couldn't take responsibility for such a valuable book.

'You could have sold it.'

'No, I couldn't! What sort of a person sells a gift?' she demanded, outraged. 'Would you?'

'Of course not. But I can afford as many books as I want.'

She flushed and Daniel felt a moment of regret for the low blow. He'd had a weekend from hell, followed by a lousy day at the office. His excellent PA had lost her usual cool after fending off yet another call from the persistent Lucy, and given him a verbal flaying his old headmaster would have been proud of. If that wasn't enough to drive a man to drink, he had an injured waif in his home, disturbing his peace. That same waif now looked at him with a mixture of hurt and loathing. He felt about six inches tall. Enough was enough.

He got up. 'Have you eaten?'

'I'm not hungry.'

'That's not what I asked, and I'm not prepared to have this same ridiculous conversation again. Come on. I'm starving.'

He held out a hand and waited. Laurel hesitated for a moment, apparently considering her chances of winning a fight with him. He could have told her she didn't stand a chance, but she was smart – she'd figure it out soon enough.

Daniel gave her a feral smile. 'How does pizza sound? You can eat that with one hand.'

He scored a bull's-eye with that one. She let him help her up, then withdrew her hand from his as quickly as she could and moved away. He fought a brief battle with his more basic instincts and let her go.

'OK,' she conceded. 'But no mushrooms.'

This time his smile was genuine. 'No mushrooms,' he agreed.

An hour later she pushed away her plate.

'I'm stuffed!'

'Well, considering you weren't hungry to start with, I think you've made a heroic effort,' he teased as he surveyed her empty plate.

'I wasn't hungry until you took them out of the oven. Where did you find such great pizzas?'

'A friend of mine has an Italian food business, and keeps me supplied with all his specialities. Haven't you explored the freezer? Help yourself to whatever takes your fancy.'

'I didn't wake up until lunch time today, and all I fancied was a bowl of soup.'

'Well, don't be shy – eat what you like while you're here.'

'Careful, you could come home and find the cupboards bare,' she laughed.

'Not judging by your consumption so far.'

Laurel sat back, feeling more relaxed than she had in ages.

Daniel poured himself a second glass of wine, and topped up Laurel's glass of juice. She'd declined the alcohol, knowing that she would need to take some painkillers to help her through the night.

'Your bruises are turning some interesting colours,' he observed.

'Mmm. But at least the swelling has gone down,' she touched the injured side of her face. The intent look in Daniel's eyes as he followed her action made her fingers tremble.

'How are your ribs?'

'Still sore, but it doesn't hurt to breathe now. Yesterday it hurt all the time, but now so long as I'm careful it's OK. No sudden moves, no deep breaths. It's amazing how quickly you learn when pain is involved.'

'You seem to have a remarkable capacity for healing.'

'It's my positive attitude. I'm positive that if I don't get myself sorted and find another job soon I'm going to be in serious trouble.'

'I've been thinking about that.'

'I'd rather you didn't. I don't want ...'

'I wasn't offering to cut any corners,' he interrupted. 'I was just wondering how you're going to get a P45 from the restaurant owner if he's skipped the country.'

'Oh God! I hadn't thought of that.' She frowned. 'I suppose I'll have to go on the emergency tax code until it can be sorted.'

'It sounds like you've been in similar situations before.'

'Yeah. I seem to have a knack for it.' She didn't want to go into details. She'd needed to eat, and sometimes the only options available had been dodgy to say the least. She'd thought she was doing all right at the restaurant though. She couldn't have known that the owner had cut corners with his insurance and would bail out as soon as trouble arose.

She shifted uncomfortably as he watched her. She felt like a bug under a microscope when he looked at her like that. She was relieved when he interpreted her movement as physical discomfort.

'Shall we move into the sitting room? You'll be more comfortable there, and I want to catch the news.'

She followed him, wondering why she didn't just plead tiredness and go to bed.

The news was the usual mix of political shenanigans, global conflict, and economic gloom. Laurel retrieved her book from the study and lost herself in the plot.

She didn't realise the programme was over until Daniel switched it off. He got up and walked over to the window, staring out onto the street and sipping his wine.

'So what will you do?' he asked suddenly. He didn't turn, but instead watched her reflection in the glass. 'About a job?'

Laurel's mind was still on the story. It took her a moment for his question to sink in.

'I don't know. I've made some phone calls and I'll go round some agencies as soon as I can, see what's available. I'll have to find somewhere to live as well. It'll

61

be a bit chicken and egg – without a job I can't afford rent, and without an address I can't get a job.'

'You can use this address.'

'Thanks, but …'

'Don't argue, Laurel. Just use it,' he growled.

Her sense of humour surfaced at his long-suffering tone. 'I would if I knew what it was,' she pointed out.

She saw his reflected surprise and relaxed a little.

'I'll write it down for you. So what sort of a job will you look for?'

'Anything. Something that allows for a broken wrist. And pays better than the last one. I'll turn my hand to most things – "hand" being the operative word,' she held up her one useable arm with a wry smile.

'You could wait until it heals.'

'Not an option,' she replied without hesitation. 'I won't presume on your good nature for that long.'

'Even though I've offered?'

'Even then.'

'So, any ideas?'

She shrugged. In truth she didn't have a clue. But that didn't mean she should give up before she started. 'Something will come up. If the worst comes to the worst I'll have to sell my body.'

Their eyes met in the window's reflection, hers defiant, his suddenly dark and unreadable. Laurel felt herself shrink inside.

Why had she said that? God! He must think she was a right tart!

'Maybe you should wait for the bruising to go down first,' he drawled.

'Yeah. And for my ribs to stop protesting every time I try to breathe,' she laughed, relieved he was taking it for the stupid joke it was.

'It's a thought, though,' he continued. 'You're a lovely girl under all that purple. I'm between mistresses myself at the moment. Who knows?'

Laurel didn't know what to say. She was rigid with shock. Was he winding her up, or was he serious? He was still standing with his back to her, and although she could see his face reflected in the window, she couldn't tell whether he meant what he said. She'd never, ever stoop so low as to sell herself like that, but Daniel French wouldn't know that. It hurt her that he might think that of her, that he thought so little of her that he could calmly discuss the possibility of her prostituting herself.

So, why was she even remotely tempted? Had she really sunk so low as to consider what he was suggesting?

'Yeah, who knows,' she snapped. 'But I'll try the job agencies first if that's OK with you.' She got up and headed for the door, desperate to get away from him. But as she touched the handle she paused. 'Oh, and maybe you'd better clear it with your girlfriend and her daddy before you take on a tart as well.' She saw his back stiffen, but had no desire to stay around for his reply. 'Goodnight,' she said, before heading for the stairs.

'What are you talking about?' His voice stopped her halfway up.

'Listen to your messages and ring your girlfriend.'

'What girlfriend?'

'There's more than one? Really, Daniel, how are you going to have the energy for a mistress as well? I tell you what. You stick to one woman, and I'll find myself a proper job, OK?'

The phone rang before he could respond.

'That's probably her now. You'd better not keep her waiting. She didn't sound happy this afternoon.'

Cursing, Daniel wheeled round and headed for the study. 'This conversation is not over, Laurel,' he warned.

'It bloody well is,' she muttered as she escaped to her room.

Her light was off and she was feigning sleep by the

time he came upstairs. Daniel came quietly into the room and stood by her bed. She forced herself to relax and breathe deeply and evenly. She knew he wasn't sure whether she was faking or not. But she'd learned her skills at an early age, when the choice had been between being the target of an abusive foster brother and playing dead. That bastard had liked his victims to be awake when he hit them. He liked to hear them screaming, something which Laurel had refused to do, even when he broke her wrist. He always lost interest when they were asleep.

She wondered with cool detachment how Daniel French would feel if he knew he was being compared to that monster. Oh, she knew he wouldn't physically hurt her, but she was quick to recognise that he had the power to hurt her in far more damaging ways. The pain that had seared through her at his throwaway remark about making her his mistress had been as intense as it had been unexpected. She usually held her own, confident in her ability to remain emotionally detached. But Daniel got to her, every time. She doubted if he was even aware of his power.

She waited, wishing he would give up and go.

Finally, just when she thought she might give herself away, he turned and quietly left the room.

She lay in the dark for a long time, wondering what his girlfriend looked like, and how she could put up with being treated so casually by a man like Daniel French. When Laurel eventually drifted into sleep, she dreamt that she was standing out in his garden in the middle of winter, shivering in the cold wind. Inside the house she could see Daniel with a woman, kissing her and stroking her. Suddenly he turned and looked straight at Laurel, his eyes cold, before he turned his back on her and led his woman away from the window.

In her dream Laurel cried.

Laurel was waiting for him when he arrived home late the following evening. He looked surprised when she opened the study door and greeted him. She was nervous, not knowing whether he would want to carry on where they had left off last night. As far as she was concerned, she'd drawn a big black line under the whole horrible conversation and she wouldn't be the one to bring it up. Instead she summoned up a polite smile.

'Hi,' he said, his expression guarded. 'Can't sleep?'

She shook her head. 'It's getting easier, especially with the extra pillows thanks. No ... I ... er ... needed to ask you something.' She hated this. If she could have avoided him she would have done. But he had something she needed.

Daniel raised his eyebrows, obviously taken aback that she was willing to swallow her pride and ask for anything.

'Ask away.'

'Can I have a spare key?'

'A key?'

'Yes. Otherwise I can't get back in if I go out.' And if he made a habit of coming home this late, she'd freeze to death on his doorstep – if the police didn't move her on first. 'I'll return it when I leave,' she told him, starting to feel even more uncomfortable under his frowning scrutiny.

He shook his head. Laurel braced herself for his refusal. Of course he wouldn't want some stranger having a key to his house.

'I'm sure you will. I'm just wondering how to apologise to you for not thinking of it myself,' he said.

This time it was Laurel's eyebrows which headed skywards.

'It's no big deal,' she responded. 'If you usually live alone it probably didn't occur to you.'

'That's exactly it. I'm sorry, Laurel. I hadn't intended to keep you prisoner here. I'll dig out a key and leave it for you in the kitchen.'

'Thanks.' She hesitated. 'Have you eaten?'

'Getting in first tonight, Laurel?' he teased.

'Thought I might give it a try,' she grinned, relieved that they seemed to be back on an even keel. After last night she'd been convinced she'd be out on her ear for sure. Maybe she and Daniel had more in common than she thought. She could never hold on to an argument for long. Life was too short to bear grudges. She liked him all the more for the fact that he seemed to be the same.

'I raided your freezer and had some fantastic lasagne. There's plenty left.'

'I'm tempted,' he said. 'But not tonight. I had a working dinner.'

So he hadn't been out with his girlfriend.

'Oh. OK. I'll finish it off tomorrow. Unless you want me to ...'

'I don't need you to cater for me, Laurel,' he cut her off. 'You're a guest, not a servant. Anyway, my schedule varies so much that I rarely eat at home. Don't bother offering to clean either – someone will be in tomorrow to do that as usual.'

He'd been doing all right for a minute there. But when he'd looked at her and said '*I'm tempted*', she had felt it right down to her toes and started to worry. Then his cool dismissal of her tentative offer of help made her feel particularly useless. One step forward, three steps back. *Keep it up, Mr French*, she thought, *and I'll be out of your hair quicker than you can wash it*.

'Fair enough,' she responded coolly. 'I'll leave you in peace. Goodnight.'

'Are you going to bed?'

'That's the idea. It is midnight.' And this Cinderella needed to get away from the Prince before she made even more of a fool of herself, she thought.

He looked at his watch.

'Of course. Sleep well.'

She hesitated on the first step.

'You too. You look tired.'

'Concerned for my welfare, Laurel?' he asked softly.

'I just ... You ...'

'Don't hold back,' he mocked, coming to stand at the bottom of the stairs.

She looked directly into his mocking eyes and scowled.

'I apologise if my natural concern for someone who's been kind to me is unwelcome.'

He ran a hand through his dark hair in a gesture which was becoming so familiar to her, and he blew out an impatient breath.

'Don't. We agreed, didn't we? No apologies. Anyway, you're right. I am tired.'

'You look like hell,' she said softly.

But that wasn't the whole truth. Her fingers itched to reach out and stroke his cheek, to feel the rasp of his late-night beard. By the morning he would be clean-shaven again, but now he looked like a pirate. A dangerous, sexy pirate.

'I know I said don't hold back, but leave me some illusions,' he laughed.

'OK. I'll shut up.' She smiled. 'Sleep well.'

'You too. Goodnight.'

She was aware of his eyes on her every step she took. When she reached the sanctuary of her bedroom she wondered whether she would dream of him again.

Chapter Five

Daniel received a call from Florence at his office late on Friday afternoon.

'Florence,' he smiled. 'How lovely to hear from you! Your voice is a balm to my stressed out mind.'

'It's not like you to admit to stress, Daniel. Is everything all right? How's your house guest?'

'Florence, Florence,' he mocked. 'Having manoeuvred me into taking the girl in, are you actually feeling guilty?'

'Not at all, my dear, but I am aware that you may both need to make some adjustments and compromises in order to rub along together. Something which I think will be to the benefit of both of you.'

Daniel wasn't sure what possible benefit it could bring either of them. Knowing that Laurel Park was sleeping just yards from his bed had given him sleepless nights. He'd done his best to avoid her for most of the week, and his work schedule had given him a valid excuse for that. But just the knowledge that she was living under his roof was unsettling. Not that he would admit such a thing to his godmother.

'Actually, my stress levels have nothing to do with Laurel. She's no trouble.' *So long as I'm not within fifty feet of her.* 'She's busy looking for another job, and I've been tied up in meetings all week. No, you've simply caught me at the end of a very long week, and I've just received a message that the firm I booked to cater for my dinner party tomorrow night has cancelled. I've got half a dozen guests arriving and there doesn't seem to be decent catering firm available in the whole of London.' He sighed. 'I was about to start ringing some restaurants to see if I can book at table at such late notice. It's a shame, because I wanted to bring these people together in private.'

'But Daniel, darling, the solution's right under your nose. You must get Laurel to organise your dinner.'

'She's got a broken wrist, Florence. And even with her experience as a waitress, I doubt she's capable of cooking the sort of dinner I had in mind.'

'I hadn't forgotten, my dear. I didn't say that she should do everything, merely that she should organise it. Don't forget that she and her friends are in the trade, so to speak. Young Christopher is a talented young chef. He'll cook, and Joanne can serve.'

'And what will Laurel do?'

'Anything she can, I imagine. If she's still looking for work, she'll be aware of how much you've helped her. This will be an opportunity for her to give you something in return.'

Daniel had a sudden, vivid memory of Laurel declaring that she'd even consider selling her body. His own reacted with embarrassing eagerness at the thought that there were several ways he would welcome getting 'something in return' from the blonde beauty who had invaded his home and his desires so reluctantly. He gritted his teeth as he stamped down on his wayward thoughts and focussed on Florence's suggestion.

'You really think it will work?' he asked.

'Of course! They're all bright young people. Give them a chance, Daniel, that's all they need.'

'I'll think about it,' he conceded, an idea forming in his mind. He didn't have a great deal of faith that Laurel and her friends could pull off a stylish dinner party, but it was beginning to occur to him that his house guest might be able to help him in another way, if he could persuade her. He might just take a chance on the dinner in order to set the scene for what he really wanted her to do for him.

By the time he arrived home, he'd changed his mind several times. Laurel was perfect for the task – she'd made it clear she didn't want to get involved with him, but at the same time her independent soul was desperate to earn her keep. She could solve what was becoming a serious problem for him without there being any danger of her expecting anything more from him.

But on the other hand, there was an undeniable spark between them that could make this plan dangerous. He'd successful ignored the sexual tension between them since the moment they met (just as he now ignored the sleepless nights he spent fighting against it), mainly by striving to be out of the house as much as possible. But she'd drawn him home. He had found himself finding excuses to go home during the day – once to collect some forgotten files; and just yesterday he'd rushed back to pick up a change of clothes before a dinner meeting, despite the fact that he had a perfectly adequate suit and shirt hanging in a closet in his office for that very purpose.

No, it was a stupid plan. And Laurel's sense of self-preservation would guarantee that she would turn him down flat. It was obvious to him that despite her bravado, she was unnerved by anything that had the vaguest sexual connotation. She came out fighting – either mocking or aggressive. But Daniel was beginning to realise that it was all one big bluff. He suspected that Laurel Park might still be sexually untouched, despite her streetwise attitude. Either that or some selfish fool had hurt her. She guarded herself carefully, avoiding physical contact, and retreating in haste whenever the attraction between them flared. It was definitely a stupid plan.

And yet ... He did need the sort of help she could provide, and she did seem to have this overdeveloped independent streak that meant she was desperate to pay her way. And maybe this would give him the chance to get the damned woman out of his system.

Laurel was surprised to see Daniel home so early.

'Hi! Are you off out again?' He'd stopped only long enough for a shower and change of clothes the night before, and she'd been asleep before he returned.

'Not tonight.'

'Oh.' She hesitated. 'Would you like a cup of tea?'

'No thanks,' he replied. 'But I do need your help with a couple of things.'

She stopped in the middle of reaching for the kettle.

'Really?' She smiled and sat at the table, waiting for him to join her. She thought he looked tired. Maybe he was having trouble sleeping as well?

'I spoke to Florence today,' he said as he sat down opposite her. 'She believes that you and your friends can get me out of a bind this weekend. I've invited some people here for dinner tomorrow, and caterers have let me down.'

'And Florence suggested we could step in?' she asked casually, trying to hide her excitement. *God Bless Florence!*

'Yes.'

His curt tone reined in the adrenaline which had begun to surge through her. *How did he do that?* He managed to deflate her with one syllable.

She rested her elbows on the table and her chin on her good hand and gave him a cool smile.

'But you're not so sure that a couple of waitresses and a cook from a greasy spoon can pull it off.'

He hesitated, meeting her gaze with a challenge in his own.

'I don't know. Can you?'

'Yeah, we can. But the only way to prove it to you is for you to let us get on with it.' Her own eyes sparked back at him as she spoke, their message meeting his challenge and raising the stakes. 'Think you can trust us?'

'I can always take them to a restaurant.'

'Coward,' she taunted. 'Go on, live dangerously! Even if you can't take my word for it, you should at least trust Florence's judgement. She's been eating at the restaurant for weeks. She told Chris he was wasted there, and she was right.'

She held her breath as he considered. Laurel wondered whether she'd gone too far, calling him a coward. But she wanted to goad him, to force him to give in and let them do this for him. All three of them needed to do something after a week of fruitless searching for work, and she especially needed to be able to help Daniel French after everything he had done for her. She was aware that, with every day she remained jobless, her debt to the man grew. It was important for her to make some contribution which might start in some small way to redress the balance.

'Very well. Get me a menu for approval within the hour, and I'll make a decision then.'

She gave him a dazzling smile.

'You won't be disappointed.'

'I sincerely hope not, Laurel. I have a lot depending on this dinner, and the last thing I want to have to worry about is what's coming out of my kitchen.'

He was almost at the door when Laurel remembered.

'Daniel?'

He turned. 'Yes?'

'You said you had a couple of things I could help you with. What was the other one?'

'We'll discuss it later,' he declared. 'Right now I need you to sort out that menu.'

Within the hour it was settled. Daniel approved the ambitious menu Chris had suggested, despite his doubts. Florence and Laurel were so sure he could do it, that Daniel decided he'd give the lad a chance. If he failed, Daniel would have to apologise to his guests and explain that his usual caterers had let him down. If he succeeded, they would all win.

Laurel got busy, ordering much of the food online using his credit card. Chris and Jo would shop for the rest in the morning after collecting some cash from him. Daniel dealt with the drinks himself, wanting to ensure that at least his guests would have no cause to complain about the quality of the wines served.

'Are you absolutely sure you can pull this off?' he'd asked.

'Yes. Trust me. We don't want to fall flat on our faces any more than you want to. Chris is a great chef, and Jo and I have both done silver service – we've even got the uniforms. Your guests won't know the difference.'

She'd held her breath, waiting for him to decide. She really needed him to let her do this. Not only did they need the work, but she also needed to do something for Daniel after everything he was doing for her. Not to mention that having something to do, if only for the next twenty-four hours, would help her combat the growing frustration and boredom that were threatening to overwhelm her.

'OK,' he'd said eventually. 'But Jo will have to serve on her own.'

Laurel couldn't believe how much that hurt.

'I know I don't look wonderful, but a bit of make-up will stop me frightening children and animals,' she made light of it.

'I know that,' he'd responded impatiently. 'I'm not worried about your appearance.'

Don't hold back, she thought bitterly. *Let me know how little I matter, why don't you?*

'Well, I'm coping fine with this,' she held up her plastered arm. 'I can balance plates on it, no problem.'

He shook his head. 'Laurel, Jo will cope with it. I don't want you to serve my guests. I want you to eat with us.'

'Why?' she asked, confused. He'd spent a week avoiding her, so why did he suddenly want to sit her at a table with his friends?

74

'I need a hostess.'

She took a step back, shaking her head. 'Oh no. I'm a waitress.'

'Not at the moment, you're not.'

'Don't hold back,' she snapped. 'Tell me to my face I'm useless, why don't you?'

'You're far from useless,' he mocked. 'Stop feeling sorry for yourself. You want to help, so help. I need a hostess, not an extra waitress.'

'But ...'

'Take it or leave it. Your friends cook and serve, you act as hostess. Or I can simply book a table at a restaurant and take my friends out.'

'What about your girlfriend?'

'Ah, yes. My alleged girlfriend. We need to talk about that.'

'It's none of my business,' she denied. 'I'm just saying you've already got a hostess, and you don't need me frightening animals and children.'

He laughed. 'You just told me you wouldn't do that.'

'Yeah, well, that's when I thought I'd be in the background, not bloody centre stage,' she grumbled, not wanting to enjoy his amusement.

He shook his head, still smiling.

'First, there is no girlfriend.'

Laurel looked sceptical.

'The call you heard was from a very persistent young woman who is desperate to please her boor of a father by snagging a rich husband that he approves of. For some reason they've picked on me, regardless of the fact that she's too young, has no mind of her own, and needs to break out and get a life. Under no circumstances would I ever ask her to be my hostess. That would be tantamount to a proposal in her eyes.' He shuddered. 'Even if I weren't determined to avoid the matrimonial trap with any woman, she'd be the last person I'd consider as a suitable wife.'

'Wow. Poor kid.'

'There's nothing "poor" about Lucy,' he snarled. 'Except her hearing when I say "no".'

Laurel laughed, slightly unnerved by how light-hearted she felt.

'And as for you frightening animals and children,' he leaned forward and lifted her chin with a gentle finger. Laurel stilled, her senses on alert. 'As I said before, you seem to have a remarkable capacity for healing. The swelling's completely gone, and your bruises are fading nicely. A few cosmetics will cover the worst of them if you're really bothered.'

'Why?'

'No reason. You don't need to cover them. My guests aren't the sort of people who would mind.'

'No, I meant why do you want me to be your hostess? You must know loads of suitable women who would be glad to do it. I'm a waitress. I won't have anything in common with a load of businessmen.'

'You might be surprised,' he smiled. 'Trust me. After all, you want me to trust you and your friends. How about a reciprocal arrangement?'

She wondered briefly whether to play dumb and ask what 'reciprocal' meant, but the knowing look in his eyes stopped her. Instead she moved back so that his hand dropped away from her face.

'What am I supposed to wear?'

His smile held quiet triumph.

'It's smart casual. I can buy you a dress in the morning.'

'No thank you.'

'You have a dress?'

'No, but Jo will have something I can borrow. She did fashion design at college.'

'So why is she a waitress?'

She shrugged. 'She decided working in a sweatshop for some prima donna designer wasn't as much fun as designing and making your own clothes. She came to work at the restaurant as a stop-gap. While she's been trying to figure out what to do next, she fell in love with Chris and got pregnant.'

'You sound like you don't approve.'

Much as she loved her friends, she was too worried for them to share their happiness about the baby. But she didn't want to talk about it either.

'It's none of my business,' she shrugged. 'But I know Jo will have something for me to wear, so you can save your money.'

'So you agree to be my hostess?'

She sighed. She was trapped. Chris and Jo were relying on her for this job, and she knew that if she turned him down Daniel would call it off. Nor would he ask her for anything again. She owed him so much, and her lack of employment so far meant that her obligation to him grew bigger every day. She was stuck between a rock and a hard place.

'OK, but don't blame me if I show you up.'

'You won't let me down,' he smiled his satisfaction. 'You have too much pride. You'll do fine.'

He was right, dammit! She'd rather chew off her own arm than let him down. But that didn't mean she was happy about it or with him. So why was she getting excited about being introduced to his friends as an equal?

'I'd better ring Jo,' she sighed.

She was just reaching for the phone when it rang. Laurel picked it up automatically.

'Hello?'

'Who is this?' a woman's voice demanded.

Laurel recognised the petulant tones immediately. The Persistent Lucy.

'This is Laurel. Can I help you?'

'I must have the wrong number. I was trying to reach … a friend.'

'Would that friend be Daniel French?' she asked, smiling as he frowned.

'Yes. Is he there?'

'Of course,' she confirmed and walked over to where he was sitting at the table and handed him the phone. But before he could take it, Laurel raised her voice, her stifled laughter giving it a husky edge. 'It's for you, darling. Don't be too long talking to your friend, will you?'

For a moment Daniel looked thunderstruck, and even Laurel's exaggerated wink didn't help. He took the phone and said his name. Laurel wandered round the table and sat opposite him, enjoying his discomfort as his caller began what she gathered was a major interrogation. Daniel let her go on for a while, his answers monosyllabic, his annoyed gaze watching Laurel's mischievous sparkle. He lifted his free hand and mimicked shooting her. Laurel clutched her chest and gave her best pantomime performance of a dying swan. Daniel grunted another response, shaking his head at her a reluctant smile tugging at his firm lips.

Laurel lay her head on her arms, one eye open watching him watching her. She wanted to laugh out loud. Who would have thought the seriously rich and sexy Daniel French could share her silly sense of humour?

'Actually, Lucy, I'm afraid tomorrow's fully booked,' Daniel reached out and brushed a few tendrils of Laurel's pale gold hair off her forehead. The laughter faded from her gaze as he rested his hand on her head, his warm fingers gently massaging her scalp. 'Laurel and I have plans.'

That obviously didn't go down well. Daniel rolled his eyes and stifled a sigh, yet the soothing movement of his fingers in her hair didn't falter. He caught her eye, his expression becoming grim and determined.

Laurel frowned. 'What?' she asked softly.

He shook his head slightly, his gaze holding hers. 'Trust me,' he mouthed at her, his fingers moving to her lips.

'Truth be told, Lucy, you're the first to know, but Laurel and I have just become engaged. We'll be out buying her ring tomorrow.'

When she would have yelped, his hand covered her mouth. He carried on talking, holding her in place, his voice calm as she glared at him with angry eyes.

'Thank you, Lucy. I appreciate your good wishes. I'll tell Laurel. Goodbye.'

He ended the call and put the phone down on the table before he released her.

'Are you mad?' she shrieked.

He raised an amused eyebrow at her panicked expression.

'Far from it,' he denied. 'Thanks to you I may just have hit on the perfect solution to the problem of The Persistent Lucy.'

'By lying to her,' she accused. 'You're not going to marry me.'

'Of course I'm not. That's not what I said. I said we were engaged.'

'But we're not.'

'Not to be married, certainly. But so long as Lucy doesn't know that I'm safe.'

'Well, she'll know it soon enough.'

'Not necessarily,' he mused. 'We could keep the charade going for weeks if we played our cards right.'

Laurel shook her head. No one in their right mind would believe that Daniel French would go out with lowly Laurel Park, let alone get engaged to her!

'It'll never work.'

Those damned mocking eyebrows raised again.

'Why not? You're living in my house already. You'll be my hostess tomorrow night. We only need be seen around town a few times and everyone will consider it a done deal.'

'Why can't you just tell her to get lost?' she asked, exasperated. Why couldn't he see how ridiculous this idea was? And why, oh why was her stupid heart breaking at the thought that he could play with her like this? Didn't he know that the more time she spent in his disturbing presence the more she wanted him?

'Because if you disregard the annoying crush she has on me at the moment, Lucy is quite a sweet girl, and it would be kinder to maintain the charade of an engagement for a while to give her the chance to get over me and get on with her life. You'll be rescuing both of us.'

Damn him! Why couldn't he be horrible?

'It'll never work,' she protested again, trying desperately to shore up her crumbling barriers. Didn't he realise he could do far more harm to her, Laurel, that he could ever do to the pampered Lucy? She probably got knocked back by the rich tycoons her father pushed her at every week. Laurel had never met a man who could get so far under her defences before, and having to pretend to be his fiancée – his love – might well destroy her.

'What about my life?' she snapped. 'I haven't got time for this. I've got a living to make.'

'So take this job. Acting fiancée. A temporary assignment with full board thrown in.'

'It's not a job. It's a great big lie!'

Unable to sit still, she leapt up, almost knocking over her chair.

'Laurel. Calm down.'

She took a breath, wrapping her good arm around her protesting ribs as she blew it out again.

'I'm perfectly calm,' she said quietly. 'And I can't do this.'

'Please, Laurel. I know you don't like me much, but can't you help me with this? You're the only person I can trust.'

She frowned. Where on earth did he get the idea that she didn't like him? If anything, she liked him too much. Her protective instincts kicked in just in time to stop her denying his statement and humiliating herself completely.

'No one will believe it, Daniel. I'm nothing like your type of woman.'

He regarded her steadily. 'Maybe not.'

She noticed he didn't deny that she wasn't his usual type.

'That's probably in our favour,' he continued. 'I've said so many times that I wouldn't marry, that they'll expect someone quite extraordinary to have made me change my mind.'

Laurel felt her jaw drop. *Extraordinary? Had he just called her extraordinary?*

'I'm not ...'

'You're very different from the women I usually mix with. Everyone will believe it's a case of opposites attracting. Which will make it easier to explain why our engagement comes to an end in a few weeks' time – our differences will make a perfect excuse for us to break up. But by then young Lucy will have moved on.'

Laurel felt cold all over. *And how will young Laurel cope?* she wanted to ask. *How will she manage to move on?*

'Come on, Laurel, be a sport. I really need your help with this.'

She closed her eyes, realising that she could get out of this by simply telling him that Lucy wasn't the only stupid girl who had a crush on him. He would run a mile. But Laurel doubted she would ever get over the humiliation.

On the other hand, she owed him so much. Without him, she'd be starving on the streets right now. She really didn't have a lot of choice, did she? And she would be doing The Persistent Lucy a favour too. She hadn't met the other woman, but she had a pretty good idea how she felt. And if Daniel French truly meant it when he said he would never marry, then they both needed to be cured of their obsessions. With any luck, pretending to be his fiancée would help Laurel. Spending more time with him would let her build up some immunity to him. Maybe, seeing him with his posh friends, being reminded of his arrogance that had so annoyed her when they met, would surely speed her towards a cure. *Wouldn't it?*

Against her better judgement, Laurel found herself agreeing to be Daniel French's temporary fiancée.

Chapter Six

She had a bad night, disoriented by hazy, disturbing dreams, and in the morning, Laurel staggered out of bed and headed for the shower. The persistent ringing of the door-bell brought her running downstairs after hastily pulling on joggers and a sleeveless T-shirt over her damp body. She assumed Daniel had already left for the office. It wasn't until she was halfway down the stairs, and he appeared in the hall below, that she remembered that it was Saturday. He smiled up at her, seemingly oblivious to her blushes. He looked incredibly sexy in a navy towelling robe, revealing a sprinkling of soft dark hair on his chest, his strong legs and tanned feet bare.

'Good timing,' he said. 'It's Lucy. I thought she'd do something like this.'

Oh God! So it hadn't been a dream!

'Just follow my lead. We need to make it plain that we're a couple.'

'This won't work,' she said as she reached the bottom on the stairs. 'We don't even like each other!'

Daniel said nothing, but grasped her shoulders and pulled her towards him, kissing her thoroughly. As soon as his lips touched hers she went up in flames. Lost in pure sensation, Laurel clung to his broad shoulders, sure her legs wouldn't hold her if she let go. She could feel that heat of his skin through her thin top, was aware of the sculpted outline of his chest and leg muscles. She didn't even notice the bell ringing again in short impatient bursts until he drew back a little. She stared up at him, her green eyes glazed with passion and confusion.

'You may not like me, Laurel,' he said softly when his lips released hers. 'But right now you look like a woman who's been well-loved. All you need to do is play along and we'll be fine.'

He kept his arm around her waist and Laurel found herself being drawn gently but firmly towards the door. She stood at his side, red-faced and breathless, hating him and hating herself, as an immaculately-dressed young woman stepped over the threshold. She spotted Laurel clamped to Daniel's side, her hair mussed, her lips moist and swollen from Daniel's kisses, and stopped dead, her perfectly made-up face paling in shock.

'Lucy,' Daniel smiled. 'How nice to see you! Come in out of the cold. Laurel and I just got up. Would you like to join us for breakfast?'

'So it's true,' she said, suddenly looking very young.

For a moment, Laurel thought the girl was going to cry, and she felt like the lowest of the low. Did Daniel really think he was doing anyone a favour with this ridiculous charade?

'Look I …' she began.

'Yes, I'm afraid so,' Daniel interrupted, his voice gentle, even as his grip tightened on her waist. 'I knew the moment I met Laurel that she was special. I tried to fight it for a while, but I know I'm the luckiest man on earth now that she's agreed to be mine.'

Laurel closed her eyes, wanting to scream. How could he say that? She was nothing to him!

'Daniel, don't,' she begged. 'We can't …'

He turned her to face him, placing a finger on her lips. She glared up at him. He kissed her firmly, frying her brain cells once again, and then pulled her head to his shoulder so that he had access to her ear. Laurel opened her eyes to see their reflection in the mirror behind him. He looked like a lover whispering sweet nothings when in fact he was growling 'Behave!'

A movement to the side of her line of vision caught her attention and she found herself looking into the reflection of Lucy's wounded eyes. It was too much.

'You're a bastard!' she snarled softly back into his ear, whilst pulling viciously at the hair on his chest, where he'd trapped her hands.

He let her go immediately, his smile strained, even as his eyes promised retribution.

She turned away from him, and faced Lucy. She was ready to end this now, but as she opened her mouth to speak, Daniel slid a gentle hand across her shoulder and down her arm. Lucy's eyes followed the movement, her mouth trembling. Laurel realised that, no matter how angry she was at Daniel for putting her in this situation, it wasn't fair to make Lucy feel any worse by bluntly telling her the truth. It would be humiliating, and she had a feeling that the young woman might never get over it.

'Why don't I make Lucy some coffee, darling, whilst you go and make yourself decent,' she suggested through clenched teeth.

Daniel gave her a sharp look, but he must have felt the fight go out of her, because he squeezed her arm gently and let go.

'All right, my sweet. I'll be back in a minute.'

Laurel breathed a sigh of relief at his easy acquiescence, but regretted letting her guard down when he leaned down and placed a lingering kiss on her lips.

'Stop that!' she swatted at him, narrowly missing doing him serious damage with her cast. She really couldn't take much more of this without collapsing into a gibbering, lust-filled heap at his feet. 'Go!'

'Yes ma'am!' He grinned at her, unrepentant, before sending Lucy a playful wink and taking the stairs two at a time.

Laurel glared after him. He was whistling, for God's sake! Shaking her head she turned to the girl who had witnessed their performance – for that was all it was, wasn't it?

'I'm really sorry about this …' she began, just as Lucy spoke.

'I'm so sorry.'

'What have you got to be sorry about?'

'I shouldn't have come. You two need to be alone.'

'Oh no!' she denied quickly. 'Daniel and I have had quite enough time alone for the moment.' *Believe me.* 'Anyway, I wanted to meet you. You're the first of Daniel's friends to call since I've been here.' *And I need some time to build up a good head of steam to blast him with next time he touches me. If I don't shoot him down in flames, I'm dead in the water.* She winced as her addled brain mixed metaphors and left her feeling stupid.

She led Daniel's guest into the kitchen and busied herself making coffee, talking about nothing in particular as Lucy sat quietly at the kitchen table looking miserable. Gradually, Laurel's inconsequential chatter seemed to get through, and Lucy's curiosity got the better of her. She asked Laurel how she'd hurt her wrist.

'And your face – is that … bruising?'

Laurel nodded, lifting her hair away from her face to reveal the technicolour marks under her skin. 'It's not too bad now, but you should have seen it last week. I looked a fright.'

'You weren't … you weren't attacked, were you?' Lucy asked, looking horrified at the thought.

'No, nothing like that. If a man tried to do this to me, I'd have given as good as I got, believe me.' Laurel smiled, warming to the girl. She didn't acknowledge that she'd learnt that lesson the hard way a lifetime ago. 'I stupidly got in the way of a runaway lorry. I just wasn't quick enough to dodge that one.'

Lucy frowned. 'But didn't I hear something about Florence …?'

'Do you know Florence? Yes, she was there. We managed to get her out of the way, thank God!'

The younger girl looked at her with wide eyes. Laurel wondered how she'd ever got the impression that Lucy was a sophisticated woman. She was just a kid, really.

'You saved her life?'

Laurel shook her head. 'Nothing so dramatic. Daniel ...'

'Can confirm that she did, and it was *very* dramatic,' he declared, walking into the room and making a beeline for her. He was freshly showered and shaved and looked good enough to eat in chinos and a polo shirt. Laurel read the intent in his eyes and forestalled him by handing him two mugs of hot coffee. She wanted no more kisses. They were far too dangerous! Daniel inclined his head in silent acknowledgement of her evasion tactics, his grey eyes mocking, and went to join Lucy at the table. Laurel took her time pouring another drink, then stayed where she was, leaning against the counter as Daniel gave his guest a highly exaggerated report of the accident. He made her sound like Superwoman, flying to the rescue.

'Oh stop it!' she scolded, laughing to hide her embarrassment. 'Don't listen to him, Lucy. I just gave Florence an almighty shove, then managed to lose my balance instead of getting out of the way like anyone with any sense would have done.'

'But you could have been killed!' Lucy protested.

'But I wasn't,' she replied firmly.

'No, she wasn't,' said Daniel, his expression sombre. 'But how I didn't have a coronary right there and then I'll never know. I thought I'd lost her.'

Laurel knew he was talking about Florence, but of course sweet, young, gullible Lucy believed exactly what Daniel had wanted her to believe. Laurel felt lower than a snake as she watched her absorb what he said, and the genuine anguish in his expression. She hated witnessing the death of the girl's romantic dreams. Everybody needs dreams.

She didn't know who was likely to blub the loudest over that performance – Lucy for her disappointment, or Laurel for sheer frustration and temper! She was saved from finding out by another blast of the doorbell, this time announcing the arrival of Chris and Jo. Lucy used their arrival as her excuse to escape – probably to spend the day crying her eyes out, the poor girl.

Laurel wanted to rant and rave at Daniel, but as soon as Lucy had gone he reverted to his usual cool, urbane self. In front of her friends he was polite and distant as usual, obviously expecting to take the wind out of the sails of her anger. Well, it wasn't going to work!

'That wasn't nice,' she hissed at him as the others helped themselves to coffee at his suggestion.

'No, but necessary. I'm grateful to you, Laurel. It was a great idea, and we're actually doing Lucy a big favour with this.'

'Are you saying it was my idea?'

He smiled, enjoying her irritation.

'Of course. You started it after all, with your playacting when she called last night. It was inspiring. I just ran with it.'

'I was trying to wind you up, you idiot!'

He laughed. Chris and Jo looked up, no longer pretending they weren't interested in what was going on between the two of them.

'I know that. But you should know by now that I'm far from an idiot. You presented me with a perfect opportunity and I took it. Now we're set on course to deal with the problem of The Persistent Lucy once and for all. It shouldn't take long – a couple of weeks at the most.'

'You really are a bastard, Daniel French! All right, I'll go along with it. But only because Lucy is a sweet girl who deserves better than a rat-bag like you!'

'Does this mean the party's off?' asked Chris, looking fed up.

'No, it doesn't.' Daniel's steely gaze dared her to contradict him.

She was tempted. Oh how she was tempted! She felt angry and guilty. And she felt aroused. That was the worst of it. It had all been a game for him, but just a touch of his lips and hands, and it had become very, very real to Laurel. Now, when she was so completely confused and hungry for more, he was able to revert to normal as though it had meant nothing!

She turned on her heel and headed out of the room.

'Where are you going?' he asked.

To wash your scent off me. And to make myself decent. Although thanks to you, there's a good chance I may never feel decent again.

'If we're going to make a success of this dinner party, we've got work to do,' she called over her shoulder. 'Jo, did you remember to bring a dress for me?'

'Of course!' Jo replied cheerfully. 'I brought a few for you to try on.'

'Right. Bring them up.'

'Do I get to approve?' Daniel called after them as they clattered up the stairs.

'No, you bloody don't!' she yelled. 'You play your part, Mr French, and I'll play mine.'

A door slammed. Daniel turned to the young man at his side and grinned. 'Women, eh?'

Chris shrugged. He hadn't seen Laurel so worked up in a long time. Most people ran for cover when she lost her rag like that. This guy just laughed. He wondered if he should warn him, then shrugged again. What the hell! He was here to cook a dinner. The rest was nothing to do with him.

'Yeah, mate,' he agreed. 'Can't live with 'em, can't live without 'em. We must be bloody mad.'

A few minutes before seven o'clock Daniel knocked on Laurel's door.

'Are you ready?' His enquiry was met with silence.

He went to knock again, just as she opened the door.

'About as ready as I'll ever be,' she informed him. 'Will I do?'

Daniel stared at the vision in front of him, shock rendering him speechless. Black silk outlined her gentle curves, making her creamy skin glow like porcelain. A delicate wrap was draped artfully over one arm, concealing her cast. Her green eyes, enhanced by expertly applied make-up, challenged him, her chin at a pugnacious angle as she waited for him to speak. When he didn't, the angle changed as her lips – those luscious lips that he'd kissed just this morning – tightening into a thin line.

'I told you this was a stupid idea,' she hissed, going to shut the door.

Daniel snapped to attention and put out a hand to prevent her from slamming it in his face.

'Not so fast! We've got guests arriving at any minute. Come on down.'

'I can't do it. I told Jo it wouldn't work, doing me up like a dog's dinner.'

Daniel followed her into the room and turned her to face him. He couldn't believe that she should feel so insecure about how she looked. Even with her present belligerent expression she looked wonderful. Exquisite. In truth he would rather ignore the fact that people were arriving downstairs. If he had a choice he would prefer to spend the evening demonstrating to this extraordinary creature just how desirable she was. He wanted to run his fingers into her beautifully arranged hair and free its pale golden softness to flow – preferably against his pillows. He wanted to run his hands over the molten silk of her dress and peel it away to reveal the warm skin beneath.

But most shocking of all, Daniel wanted to gather her

close and just hold her. To be the man to take away her insecurities and to release the vibrant woman that he'd glimpsed from time to time over the past week. The woman who deserved to be loved without reserve.

Hell! What was he thinking? He must be going crazy! Whatever mysteries Laurel Park had hidden beneath her gorgeous exterior were of no interest to him. OK, so he lusted after her – who wouldn't? But he sure as hell didn't want to think about love and Laurel in the same breath! She was a means to an end – to get rid of one persistent woman-child – and he had no intention of engaging his emotions. He wanted to bed her, he couldn't deny it, but nothing more. He didn't do love. He needed to remember that, no matter how breathless and aroused she made him.

'You look fine,' he snapped impatiently. 'Come down and have a drink before they arrive. It'll calm you down.'

'No, I'll change into my uniform. There's no way I can pull this off.'

'Don't be tiresome.'

'And don't you patronise me! You've got a peer of the realm, an MP, and a millionaire businessman coming to dinner. That's no problem for you because you're old mates. But what will your friends say if they knew I'm a homeless, jobless waitress?'

'Tell them and find out,' he challenged. 'But my guess is that you're standing there panicking and hating my guts because we both know you wouldn't have the nerve.'

'Why would I expose myself to their pity, or contempt? That's not cowardice, that's survival!'

'So don't tell them. Either way suits me. Just so long as you get rid of that dog-in-the-manger attitude and start acting the part.'

'God, I hate this!' she muttered, her shoulders drooping in defeat.

Daniel hid a smile. For all her protests, she could pull this off. He'd called her bluff and won. In fact, she didn't know it yet, but his guests would be delighted to know her background; nor would they treat her with anything but the highest respect. Maybe he was being cruel, keeping her in the dark, but a part of him was unwilling to make it too easy on her when he was struggling to keep his distance from his disturbing houseguest.

'You really are a little coward, aren't you, Laurel Park?' he taunted.

She stilled, her fists clenching. 'I'm no coward.'

'Oh yes you are. You hide behind that great big chip on your shoulder. You pretend to be full of it, ready to take on the world. But here's your chance to do a simple favour and be my hostess for a small dinner party, and you want to rush back into the shadows and play the servant instead of using your brain and your wits to show the world that Laurel Park can do anything she sets her mind to.'

'But I look awful.'

'No you don't. You look fine.'

'Liar. Your face said it all when I opened the door.'

He shook his head. Maybe it would be better to let her go on thinking he didn't like how she looked. It would be safer for him that way, certainly. But he couldn't do that to her. He stepped close and put his hands on her bare shoulders. He felt her trembling and couldn't resist stroking the soft skin.

'You misinterpreted. That chip must be affecting your eyesight as well.'

She glared at him, but said nothing.

'I was surprised, Laurel. But not in a negative way. You look exquisite. The perfect hostess.'

It was her turn to look shocked. Daniel smiled as she fought an inner battle, not sure whether to believe him or not, or how to react. He kept his gaze steady and sincere as she regarded him with suspicion.

'You're supposed to say "thank you" when someone compliments you.'

'Thank you.' She smiled suddenly.

Daniel's hands tightened on her shoulders. The urge to kiss her had him pulling her closer. Laurel saw his intent in his eyes, but did nothing to stop him. Her green eyes looked huge, urging him closer. But before their lips touched, the doorbell rang, heralding the arrival of their guests. He closed his eyes briefly, and stepped away.

'Saved by the bell,' she laughed breathlessly. 'Thanks for the vote of confidence, boss, but don't go overboard, eh?' She stepped away from him. 'I'm all right now. This is just a job. I can do this. No problem. Let's get on with it, shall we?'

Daniel swallowed down angry words as he watched her walk away. *Did she really think he was as crass as to kiss her to get her co-operation to do her job as his hostess? Didn't she realise she could turn him on with just a look, a smile?*

She turned at the top of the stairs and waited for him to join her. Below he heard Jo greeting his guests and taking their coats. Daniel didn't have time to worry about his desire for this infuriating woman right now.

'OK,' he said as he took her hand and threaded it through his arm. 'Let's get this show on the road.'

Daniel had introduced her to his guests over aperitifs in the drawing room. He'd kept her close, holding her hand against his arm to prevent her from escaping, which she'd tried to do the moment they'd reached the bottom of the stairs.

Robert Habgood-Starck, a baronet and old school friend of Daniel's, and his sister, the Honourable Pamela, were both tall and stick thin. She was Laurel's idea of a 'Sloan Ranger' – sophisticated yet jolly, and frightfully posh. Laurel couldn't imagine having anything in common with her, and braced herself. Her experience of Pamela's type, as a skivvy paid to clean their homes, had been demeaning. But Pamela greeted her with grace and friendliness, and complimented her on her dress.

'Thank you,' Laurel said, her smile genuine for the first time since she'd entered the room. 'A friend of mine designed and made it.'

'Well you must give me her number. I've got such an awkward shape I have a devil of a job finding the right clothes.' She grimaced. 'I'm too tall, that's the problem. And no matter how much I eat, I can't seem to develop any curves.'

Laurel looked at her expensive silk trouser suit. 'Oh but you're lovely! Like a model!'

Robert laughed. 'A model? Oh no, not Pammy. Mother always said she walked like a man.'

Pamela laughed too, but not before she aimed a good dig with her elbow at her brother's ribs.

'Well I know my friend will be delighted to make you some clothes, Pamela,' Laurel said. Now was not the time to tell her that their waitress for the evening was the wonder-worker. Both she and Jo knew that they wouldn't recognise her later. No one took any notice of the hired help.

From the corner of her eye, she could see Jo topping up glasses, her face pink. Laurel smiled at her as she approached to refill her own drink. Her friend beamed at her. 'Thanks, Laurel,' she whispered.

Maybe this evening wasn't going to be so bad after all!

The second couple were completely different. David Thurgood was a bluff city banker, and his elegant wife Eloise was at least fifteen years younger than her well-padded husband. She seemed strained, almost brittle, against her husband's determined cheerfulness.

The final guests were household names – an outspoken MP, Hugo Greyson, and his journalist wife Susannah. Laurel couldn't quite put her finger on what Daniel's guests would have in common other than knowing him and all of them having a lot of money. Daniel had told her that he was bringing them together in the hope that they would help Robert with a pet project.

Laurel was grateful that it was only a small gathering, and although she'd never admit it to him, she was also grateful of Daniel's presence at her side. His warmth and support gave her the confidence to play her part, smiling and chatting to these strangers who were his friends and equals. She wasn't so grateful, however, when he raised her left hand to his lips, and Pamela shrieked as she spotted the large emerald on her ring finger.

'Oh my God! Daniel French, can it be true? Has a mere woman finally brought you to your knees and been rewarded with a proposal?'

Laurel blushed, fixing a smile on her face while wanting nothing more than to disappear in a puff of smoke. It was her left wrist that was broken, yet the sight of Daniel's ring on her finger distracted everyone from the fact.

Daniel was enjoying the sensation he'd caused, accepting his friends' congratulations without a flicker of conscience. Laurel caught Jo's eye, and accepted her own friend's understanding grimace with a wry twist of her lips. She'd explained the situation to Chris and Jo this afternoon, after Daniel had taken her to an exclusive jeweller's in Hatton Garden and placed the ring on her finger. She'd tried to talk him out of buying such an expensive prop for what was essentially a short-lived charade, but he had been adamant that people would expect him to provide his bride-to-be with a suitable ring.

'Stop worrying, Laurel. I can afford it. And when this is all over, you can sell it.'

'I will not!' she argued. 'You'll take it back! I don't even see why we need to do this. Thanks to your play-acting this morning, Lucy definitely got the message.'

'Yes, but now she'll have to go home and tell Daddy, and believe me, old man Pemberton won't be so easy to fool. Until he's convinced I'm a lost cause, he'll pressure the girl to keep pursuing me. No, we need to do this properly, and that means having a very public engagement.'

Now she numbly accepted their guests' good wishes, and his tender kiss, while reminding herself that nothing about this situation was real. Nothing except the fact that every time he touched her, Daniel French demolished another layer of her hard-won defences.

When one of the men finally commented on her injury, Daniel treated them to a repeat of his explanation to Lucy, and she cringed anew. She noticed he didn't mention that she'd been clearing tables at the restaurant. Instead, he gave the impression of a man smitten. Laurel's smile was forced as she listened to him. *Just remember it's all a game*, she told herself. *It doesn't mean a thing. You're still on your own. You can't rely on anyone else.*

Laurel was relieved when she was finally seated at the head of the table, at the opposite end to Daniel. At least with six people between them he wouldn't be able to touch her. She couldn't believe that she'd let him get away with so much kissing and handling when she'd perfected any number of techniques to deter unwanted touching. But whenever he came close she was lost. She actually *enjoyed* his kisses and caresses! Even though she knew they were all a big lie, and that she meant nothing to him. Even though every other man's touch always left her cold.

She concentrated on smiling like a newly-engaged woman, fielding questions from the women about wedding plans.

'It's all happened so fast,' she said with a shy smile, 'we haven't had time to think.'

It seemed to satisfy them, and Laurel let the conversation flow around her. She was quietly thrilled, that, as each course arrived, the compliments for the chef grew ever more expansive.

'Daniel, darling, whoever you've got cooking for you tonight is a genius,' Eloise declared. 'I do hope you're going to share your discovery with us. I have a reception to organise next month and the chef I've been dealing with is being tiresome.'

'Of course. He's a young chap just starting out on his own. I'll make sure you talk to him before you leave.'

Laurel beamed at Daniel, so pleased for her friends. Tonight could be the start of great things for both of them, thanks to him. Daniel smiled back at her with perfect understanding. She felt her heart rate increase. Why, oh why did he have to be so nice, even when he was putting her in such an awkward situation? It would have been much easier to deal with him if he stayed arrogant and overbearing.

It wasn't until they were in the drawing room enjoying coffee and brandies that the conversation finally touched upon Robert's project. Laurel wasn't paying much attention at first. Her attention was instead focussed on the fact that she was sitting too close to Daniel on one of the sofas placed at right angles to the Adam fireplace. Pamela sat on the other side of him, while Robert stood talking to David and Hugo. Susannah and Eloise occupied the other sofa, apparently catching up on news of mutual acquaintances.

Laurel finished her coffee and reached forward to place the cup and saucer on the low table between the two sofas. When she leant back, she realised Daniel had slipped his arm around her shoulders. Startled, she looked up at him.

'All right?' he asked quietly.

She nodded stiffly. She knew she didn't have a hope of getting him to back off in front of his guests. She just had to remember that he was playing a part, that the soft stroke of his fingers on her bare arm meant nothing.

'You're doing fine,' he told her. 'Relax.'

She shook her head slightly. How could she relax?

97

'You have got to be joking.'

He laughed softly, and kissed her temple.

She almost whimpered. When she realised that Susannah was watching them with an indulgent smile, she blushed, getting angry with Daniel all over again.

Oh what the heck! If he wants a clinging fiancée, that's exactly what he'll get! Laurel decided, as she made herself relax against his warm body and smile up at him with adoring eyes. *Maybe if I act like a besotted fool, he'll back off.* But when he smiled back and kissed her on the lips, it occurred to Laurel that maybe he wouldn't. And if he didn't, she was in serious trouble.

She was beginning to panic, when she was distracted by something Hugo said to his companions.

'Believe me, Robert, I'm willing to try. But the public perception of them is that they're all ungrateful yobs and teenage mothers demanding handouts. Trying to help these kids is a thankless task. They don't help themselves with their anti-social behaviour and attitudes.'

'But don't you see? They need help, not punishment! Instead of ploughing money into building more young offenders' institutions, the government should be creating a society where these young people are cared for and nurtured.'

'Oh, Robert,' Pamela sighed. 'Not tonight, please! Can't you have a rest from your crusade for just a couple of hours?'

She saw Laurel frowning and shook her head.

'My dear brother isn't satisfied with his privileged lot in life and wants to make everyone else sickeningly happy,' she explained. 'He's involved with a charity which is devoted to keeping yobs off the streets by giving them drop-in centres to go and vandalise instead. Much as I applaud his need to do something, I can't help thinking he's going the wrong way about it.'

'Oh?' Laurel thought she was probably right, having

experienced her share of 'do-gooders' thinking they could solve her problems with a day at a theme park, or the chance to play expensive games on a computer. But she was aware that she was an interloper at this gathering, and kept her expression mildly interested, as befits a good hostess.

'My sister is happy to organise fundraising events, Laurel, but she refuses to get her hands dirty and meet the kids we're working with. She has no idea what some of them have been through. If she did, she'd be as passionate as I am about giving them a chance.'

'But why should she?' asked David. 'As Pamela said, you provide them with drop-in centres, and the next thing you know, they've nicked the TVs and wrecked the place.'

'That happened once, and it wasn't the kids who used the centre,' he defended. 'They were ambushed by an older gang – the very people we were trying to protect them from. Our kids are under sixteen, still being looked after in care homes. They weren't responsible for the damage.'

Laurel knew that Daniel was watching her. No doubt he could feel her tension increasing as he continued to stroke her shoulder. At first she had been stiff with annoyance at his blatant manoeuvring to play the besotted fiancé, but now her agitation was building as she listened to Robert defend his charity's work.

'What do you think, darling?' Daniel asked.

She slanted him an irritated look. 'You don't want to know,' she told him between clenched teeth.

'On the contrary. I think you've got a lot to contribute to this debate.'

Laurel looked up. She realised with dismay that she was the centre of attention. She shook her head and forced a smile. This wasn't the place or the time.

'I don't think so. I'm sure Robert's doing what he thinks is best.'

'Exactly!' exclaimed Pamela, rolling her eyes. 'He's trying his best, but as usual he hasn't got a clue!'

'Oh, and you do?' Robert laughed, starting to look annoyed.

'No, but it's obvious that the current programme isn't working, and it's grinding you down, Robert. The whole thing needs rethinking.'

'That's all very well for you to say, but what else can we do? We're trying to provide these youngsters with an alternative to hanging around the streets, to encourage them to develop hobbies ...'

Laurel couldn't help herself. *What planet were these people from?*

'Hobbies?'

She didn't realise she'd spoken out loud at first. But when the whole room went silent and looked at her she knew that she was well and truly caught out.

'I'm sorry, Robert. That was very rude of me.'

'Actually, my love, I think it was the most useful thing that's been said tonight,' said Daniel smoothly. 'So why don't you elaborate?'

She turned to meet his steady, challenging gaze. It didn't take a lot of intelligence to realise he'd set her up. And calling her 'his love' wasn't going to help him, she decided.

The mood Laurel was in, she was ready to give it to them all with both barrels!

Chapter Seven

'OK,' she agreed, her chin rising. She put her hand on his leg and pushed herself upright, at the same time pinching the inside of his thigh hard between her thumb and forefinger in punishment. She walked over to the sideboard and poured herself a brandy before turning to face Daniel's guests. She didn't look at their host, although she was aware that he'd crossed his punished thigh over his other leg and was gently massaging his abused flesh. *Serve him right,* she thought, *for setting me up like this.*

'Drop-in centres with ping-pong and crafts and video games are a waste of time. You're not preparing them for real life. All these kids have to look forward to is what those older yobs have already discovered – that if you've been brought up in care you're marked. Your schooling will have been disrupted; you won't have any roots, no support systems to fall back on. Keeping them occupied with pointless hobbies is just increasing their belief that all they're good for is sitting around waiting for handouts.'

'But surely they deserve some recreation?' Robert interrupted, his expression earnest. 'Why shouldn't they have some fun?'

'Because if you haven't got a decent education, or a roof over your head, or food in your belly, life *isn't* fun! While you're doling out "recreation and fun",' she outlined the words by tracing quote marks in the air with her fingers, 'the very people you're aiming to help are drowning. They have nothing and no one to fall back on when they're turfed out of care at sixteen. They'll be dumped in hostels and bed-sits, forced to take crap jobs because no one's bothered to find out if they have any skills or aptitude for anything better. And that's if they can find any work at all. They aren't able to get full housing benefits if they're under eighteen; have no idea how to deal with money, feed themselves, the price of clothes or anything! Most of them end up on the streets because they can't pay their rent, and with no address they become non-people. They have to go into public toilets to wash, to steal or beg for food, and have no idea whether they'll survive the night. No one will employ them except pimps and drug dealers.'

'My God!' Eloise exclaimed. 'Surely not!'

'Believe me. That's exactly what they've got to look forward to,' she insisted.

'So what would you do?' asked Daniel into the silence that followed.

She turned to look at him, her eyes blazing. He'd asked for her opinion, damn him! Did he think she was going to give some quiet, simpering answer when she was so wound up by the sheer ignorance of these people?

'Give them the skills to survive – help them stay at school or go to college so they have a chance to get a decent job; teach them the basics, like coping on a budget, cooking cheap, healthy meals; make sure they have a decent landlord who isn't going to throw them out at the first sign of a problem.'

'Oh, but that's the responsibility of the local authorities that have been caring for these children,' said Hugo. 'The government sets out clear guidelines.'

Laurel laughed. How could he be so smug? 'Yeah, and every council in the land is claiming they can't afford it, and passing the buck. They'd rather spend their money on building fancy shopping centres and office blocks, then wonder why these kids vandalise the places the first chance they get.'

'So are you saying you condone such criminal

behaviour?' asked Susannah.

'Of course not! But I understand it. If you'd been sleeping on the streets, treated like rubbish and patronised by do-gooders offering you the chance to sit and watch a video about people who had everything you didn't have and have no hope of ever getting, wouldn't you want to break a few windows?'

'So, what you're saying is,' chimed in Pamela, the light of battle in her eyes, 'who's the real criminal in this situation – the authorities who are supposed to care for them, or the young people for getting their own back?'

'Exactly!' Laurel and Pamela smiled at each other, in complete understanding. She realised she'd misjudged her completely. The Honourable Pamela was a woman she could like and respect.

'So we should just sit back and let them mug us in the streets?' asked David, a sour expression on his face. 'Thanks to these kids, no one is safe these days.'

'I'm sorry, David. I didn't realise you'd been a victim of crime,' said Laurel, her voice deceptively soft.

'What? Um, I haven't actually. But I've heard ...'

'I've heard that you're more likely to be a victim of white-collar criminals hacking into your bank account than being mugged by a kid in care,' she told him. 'Especially here in Mayfair.'

Daniel laughed. 'She's got you there, old man.'

'Absolutely!' Robert agreed.

Laurel was relieved when David gave a rueful smile.

'You're probably right,' he conceded.

'You certainly seem to have a lot of sympathy for these people. But surely we should be expecting their families to take responsibility?' asked Eloise, looking unconvinced.

'Their families are usually the problem,' said Robert explained patiently. 'If they were capable of looking after their children, the kids wouldn't be in care.'

The room fell silent for a moment as everyone absorbed

what they'd heard.

'So, how do you know so much about this, Laurel?' asked David, his voice loud as he broke into their thoughts.

Her instinctive reaction was to look at Daniel. He returned her gaze with a steady regard, as though he was telling her that it was all right to share her deepest, darkest secrets. That she would be safe.

But old habits die hard. She'd spent her life guarding her privacy. It wasn't natural for her to share so much. But the look in his eyes challenged her, even as it encouraged her and offered her his support. For a wild moment she wondered if he was playing some cruel game, setting her up for his friends' ridicule and contempt. But then her mind cleared. No. Daniel French might be a ruthless pig at times, but he wasn't deliberately cruel. She could trust him. Although the more time she spent with him, the harder it was to trust herself.

'I'm one of them,' she told them quietly, not taking her eyes off Daniel. He gave her the courage to hold her head high and tell these people the truth about her life. 'I spent sixteen years being "looked after" in children's homes and with foster families. I know exactly what it's like for those kids – and the older ones who wrecked your centre.'

'But you've done all right,' frowned Eloise. 'Why would so many of the others go off the rails?'

Laurel shook her head in denial. Daniel rose in one fluid movement and came to stand at her side, his hand seeking hers and raising it to his lips.

'That's because Laurel's a very special woman. She's smart and strong, and has too much pride to let life get her down.'

Did he really think that? No one had ever called her special before! But even as her heart soared at his words, her head was reminding her that this wasn't real. Daniel was just making people believe that he cared so that he could protect his solitary life. He didn't want anyone, especially not a little nobody like her.

'I don't know who you're working for at the moment, but I'm prepared to double what they're paying if you'll come and work for me,' said Robert. 'Pammy's right. I want to help, but I don't have clue. You, on the other hand – good grief Laurel, you're just what we've been looking for!'

Laurel laughed, not letting herself take him seriously. How could anyone offer to double someone's salary, just like that? The fact that she didn't have any salary coming in at all gave her reaction a slightly hysterical edge.

Daniel smiled. 'He means it, you know.'

Robert looked bemused. 'Of course I mean it! Will you come and work for me?'

Laurel shook her head. He didn't mean it. He couldn't.

'Doing what?' she asked. 'I'm not trained.'

'My dear girl, you've had the most valuable training in the world. You've been there. You know what they need, and how best to give it to them. You could make a tremendous difference. At least say you'll think about it?'

She blinked. *He really did mean it!* 'OK.'

'Excellent! Daniel can bring you over for lunch tomorrow and we can talk details.'

'Goodness me, Laurel,' Susannah laughed. 'What a night! A gorgeous fiancé and a new career in the same week. I do hope I'm going to get the exclusive on this for my paper.'

Laurel felt her heart miss a beat. No way would Daniel want their fake engagement paraded through the newspapers! And if these people found out how they were being fooled, she could see any possible job offer being snatched back so fast …

'Susannah, stop teasing my girl,' Daniel chuckled. 'I know full well you've just resigned from the paper to write a political thriller.'

The other woman pouted prettily as Laurel found she could breathe again.

'No one can ever keep a secret in this town,' she complained.

Oh yes they can, Laurel thought. *They most definitely can.*

'He really meant it, didn't he? He offered me a real job. It wasn't a set up?'

They had said goodbye to the last of their guests and Chris and Jo had just left in the taxi that Daniel had thoughtfully booked and paid for. Laurel almost skipped up the stairs ahead of him.

'Yes. Robert's a good man, and he wants to do what's best for those kids. I'm glad he's been smart enough to recognise that your experience gives you the sort of insight he needs to give them a better chance in life.'

When she reached the landing Laurel was close to tears. She hated crying, even though this time she was fighting back happy tears. But it didn't stop the wide smile tugging at her lips. Someone wanted *her*, Laurel Park, to help make a difference.

'But why? His life is so far removed from theirs.'

'That's the point. He inherited everything he has and feels guilty every day that he has so much when others have nothing. He's not the sort of man to sit back and ignore that. He wants to share some of his luck with others who need it.'

'I had no idea. He's a nice man.'

'Yes, but don't forget that I still need you to act as my fiancée until we can be sure young Lucy's father has accepted that I won't be making an honest woman of his little girl.'

'I don't know why you can't just be a man and tell him straight. I can't believe you're such a wuss!'

He laughed, too mellow from fine food and wine to

object to her cheek.

'Gerald Pemberton is not a man to listen to what he doesn't want to hear. No we'll just have to see this through. Now stop trying to distract me. Will you accept Robert's job offer?'

'Of course! Even if I weren't desperate to earn a living, I feel like I was made for something like this! Don't you see? If my experience means that I can help other kids – God!' She spun round, hugging herself, unable to keep still. 'It will make it all worthwhile, don't you see? Otherwise, it was all pointless, horrible ...' She stood before him, her eyes shining. 'Now I can turn it into something positive. I can even move out of here and leave you in peace.'

He smiled down at her.

'I'm pleased for you, Laurel. You'll do a great job, I know. But there's no rush to move out. You'll have to work a month in hand before you get your first pay cheque anyway.'

A month. A whole month. Did she dare? When the alternative was being alone once more, and never seeing Daniel French again, then yes, she decided, she did dare.

On impulse, she reached up and took his face in her hands, cupping one side with her good hand, and stroking the fingertips of her plastered hand down his cheek.

'Thank you,' she whispered.

'What for?' he asked. 'You did it all yourself.'

'But I wouldn't even have met Robert if you hadn't made me pretend to be your fiancée.'

All at once Laurel realised how close they were. She wondered when it had become a pleasure to reach out and touch this man, when she'd spent her life avoiding physical contact with others. She wished that the charade they had been playing could be real, that she could be his woman, his love. Without giving herself time to think she pulled his head down and reached on tiptoe to kiss him on the lips.

For a moment Daniel hesitated, and Laurel would have pulled back. Her heart missed a beat and she stiffened. *What was she doing? She never kissed anyone!* She'd tolerated his kisses earlier because she'd had no choice. Anyway, she had felt relatively safe in public, and they'd only kissed because he had asked her to do a specific job for him – to deter The Persistent Lucy. What must he think now, when she kissed him, when they were alone? She tried to step back, but Daniel's strong arms came around her body and held her close. She leaned back a few inches, staring up into his silver grey gaze. Her hand was still on his cheek, and she felt his jaw tense. She saw his pupils dilate with desire. For *her*. Her lips parted in wonder. *He really wanted her!*

She had barely formed the thought when he took her mouth in an explosive kiss. Laurel clung to him, revelling in the invasion of her mouth, matching him stroke for stroke as his tongue explored and branded. She wanted to get closer, to absorb all of him. No one else had ever made her feel like this – no one else had ever made her rejoice in the surrender of her body, in the feel of strong arms holding her, exploring her. She groaned as his mouth left her, and purred as he began to explore her throat with his lips.

'God, Laurel! You set me on fire!' his deep voice rumbled against her sensitized skin.

'I'm burning too,' she whispered. 'Oh Daniel, please.'

'Please what? Please let you go? Or something else? Tell me now Laurel, before it's too late for me to stop.'

'Please … don't stop! I … want … I need …'

Laurel found herself swept into his arms, his mouth covering hers again as he carried her into his room.

Much later, as pale fingers of the dawn began to reach across the room towards Daniel's bed, Laurel lay naked in

108

her sleeping lover's arms.

He hadn't seemed surprised that she was a virgin. Laurel felt as though he'd seen deep into her soul and known without being told that she had guarded herself for so long against the predatory males who saw a young girl without the protection of a family as fair game. From the moment he'd laid her on his bed he'd been gentle, teaching her that not every man took his pleasures selfishly. He'd made love to her slowly, until she was crying out in ecstasy and begging him to take her where she had never been before.

And he had. Oh he had! She smiled against his chest, revelling in the delicious experience of lying skin to skin with this wonderful man. She had never believed she would ever feel so safe, or so *satisfied*, in such a situation. She could feel his heartbeat, strong and steady as she nuzzled closer, luxuriating in the freedom to touch him as she had wanted to do from the moment she'd seen him at the restaurant.

With a sigh she closed her eyes, letting exhaustion finally claim her.

When she awoke again she was alone and the autumn sun filled the room with a golden glow.

The steamy residue on the en-suite bathroom mirror told her that Daniel had already showered. Her borrowed dress lay neatly folded on a chair. Laurel wondered whether Daniel was planning on coming back to bed, but the faint sound of the radio playing downstairs in the kitchen seemed to indicate otherwise.

Laurel wrapped herself in the towelling robe she'd seen him wearing only twenty-four hours ago. It was huge, and she felt surrounded by his essence as she hurried downstairs to see him.

It wasn't until she stood in the doorway of the kitchen and saw him standing by the window that she began to have second thoughts. He was fully dressed, dark hair still

109

damp from the shower, his back ramrod straight as he looked out. He obviously hadn't heard her above the noise of the radio.

He looks so alone, she thought, and suddenly she was afraid. *What if he preferred to be alone? What if last night meant nothing to him?*

As if sensing her presence, Daniel turned and saw her. He didn't smile. Laurel felt cold.

'My robe suits you,' he commented.

She pulled it tighter around her slender body.

'I'm sorry,' she sighed. 'I don't know what the form is for the morning after. Wearing this seemed like a good idea at the time.'

He put his empty coffee mug on the counter and came to stand in front of her.

'I'm sorry too. I shouldn't have left you alone. But you were sleeping so soundly I didn't think you'd be up for hours. I don't want you to feel awkward.'

I'd feel a lot less awkward if you'd put your arms around me and kiss me, she wanted to say.

She couldn't look at him. 'It doesn't matter,' she said. 'I'll go and get dressed.'

Daniel's hand on her arm stopped her.

'There's no rush.'

She did look at him then, and felt heat flood through her at the desire in his gaze. She swallowed hard. Now that she knew just how he would satisfy those desires, and how much pleasure she would gain from his lovemaking, she wanted him to look at her like that again and again.

She felt herself sway towards him and raised her face to receive his kiss. She closed her eyes as their lips met, savouring his touch. When she felt his hand slide inside the robe to cup her breast she moaned, pressing herself closer, wanting ...

Laurel almost whimpered when he withdrew, first his hand, and then his lips from her skin. But something warned her that Daniel would not want his woman to cling. Instead, she took a deep, steadying breath and stepped back, a soft smile on her moist, kiss-swollen lips.

'Coffee?' he offered, his deep voice raspy.

'Please,' she replied, moving away to sit at the table.

Laurel frowned, her teeth worrying her lower lip as he turned away to pour her drink. She didn't know what to expect from him. This felt so odd. *But then when had she ever felt completely comfortable in his presence, other than last night in his bed?* She hardly knew him after all. In fact, she'd never known anyone like Daniel French. *Was that why she found it so easy to fall in love with him?*

'Here you go.' Daniel placed a steaming mug on the table in front of her, unaware of the shock reverberating through her mind and body. 'Do you want some toast?'

'Uh, no. No thanks. This … this is fine.'

She wrapped trembling hands around the cup and stared into its depths, afraid that if she looked at Daniel he would see what her foolish heart had just revealed to her. She wasn't stupid. No matter how strong his desire for her body, he would never love someone like her. Which begged the question – what on earth was she going to do now?

Laurel was aware that Daniel was watching her, but she concentrated on taking careful sips of her drink, her eyes careful avoiding his gaze. After a moment he checked his watch, before leaning forward on his crossed arms.

'Look at me. Please.'

Startled by his soft words, she did so. She was immediately locked into his steady gaze, unable to look away. She called on years of training to keep her eyes clear and her expression neutral.

'Should I apologise? Do you regret giving yourself to me, Laurel?'

Did she? If she had the chance would she go back in time and change what had happened?

111

'No. It was … lovely.'

The corner of his beautiful mouth turned up in a rueful smile and shook his head.

'Damned with faint praise,' he mocked. 'Lovely?'

She flushed. He wanted it all, didn't he?

'Yes. Lovely, and mind blowing, and better than I ever imagined. Does that satisfy your ego? Or should I come up with a few more superlatives for you?'

'Oh I think my ego can manage with what crumbs you've dished out,' he laughed. 'After all, I only have to remember your cries of pleasure when I was inside you to know that it was so much more than your prim little mind will admit.'

She sat back, crossing her own arms, hating him for making fun of her, yet aware that his words had conjured up memories that had her nipples peaking painfully against the fabric of his robe.

'I don't know what you want from me, Daniel,' she said. 'Why don't you tell me what you expect? It might save us both a lot of grief.'

'Maybe I should have shown more restraint last night. It didn't seem to matter then that you were untouched.'

So he had noticed.

'Are you saying that *you* have regrets?' she mocked. 'Because I distinctly remember your own moans of pleasure matching mine in both volume and content. You sounded like you wanted it just as much as I did.'

'Oh, I wanted you, Laurel. Have no doubts about that. And I want you again.'

'But?' she raised a quizzical eyebrow, determined not to let him see who much his words affected her.

'But I don't do commitment,' he declared coolly. 'I don't want commitment. I have no desire to tie myself to one person, I don't want children, and I will never marry.'

'So you just want to shag, is that it?' she asked, hiding her hurt behind her streetwise bravado.

'I wouldn't have put it quite so crudely,' he responded, his voice as detached as the expression in his eyes. 'Essentially, I want to explore the attraction between us for as long as it lasts without finding that, because I'm your first lover, you've developed expectations that are never going to be realised.'

Laurel felt something shrivel and die inside her. Once again she had to face the fact that she wasn't good enough.

She got up.

'Where are you going?'

'I need to get dressed. Aren't we supposed to be going out to lunch?'

She managed to sound as cool as he, but knew that if she didn't get away from him soon she'd start throwing things.

'We need to talk about this, Laurel,' he said. 'It's foolish to leave it like this.'

'Don't worry, Daniel,' she said, using the excuse of washing up her mug to keep her back to him. 'I know the score. I won't be a problem.'

He was silent for a moment, as though he didn't believe her. Then she heard his chair scrape back as he got up and moved to join her. She stayed where she was, letting him reach out and pull her back against his chest, his warm hands on her shoulders. She closed her eyes and tipped her head back as he nuzzled her neck.

'I'm glad,' he said softly, his warm breath caressing her skin. 'We're good together, you and I. Last night was just a taster. I'm going to enjoy teaching you.'

'Was I that bad?' she laughed shakily, drowning in sensation.

'Not too bad.' His husky response sent shivers down her spine. 'In fact, you show the promise of being an extremely passionate lover. I'm going to enjoying showing you how to be even better at being very, very bad.'

With a final kiss on her temple, he reluctantly released

her.

'But as you reminded me, we are expected at Robert's for lunch. If we're going to be on time we'd better get a move on. His place is out of town. Can you be ready in half an hour?'

Laurel felt empty as he stepped away. He had played her body like a finely tuned instrument. She had felt his gently touches vibrate through her senses, leaving her trembling in anticipation. Yet he'd been able to step back as though it had meant nothing.

'OK,' she agreed, unwilling to look at him, and fled to the sanctuary of her room.

Her unslept-in bed mocked her as she sat down at the dressing table and stared at her reflection in the mirror. She didn't look any different, but she would never be the same again. In just one short week in Daniel French's world she had broken the most important rule of all – she had let herself need someone.

For a few brief hours she had known utter happiness, and she'd allowed herself to believe that it could be real. But Daniel's little speech just now had reminded her that life wasn't like that. Happiness was just a foolish illusion. She could depend on no one but herself for her emotional wellbeing.

But the physical? Well, she couldn't regret sleeping with him. She hadn't known that such pleasure was possible until she'd found it in Daniel's arms.

She wanted more of it, and she suspected that she wouldn't find it with another man.

Could she guard her fragile heart enough to take what he was offering – a chance to explore this amazing chemistry between them and to experience mind-blowing sex for as long as Daniel wanted her? She closed her eyes against the fear she could see lurking in their depths. How long would it be before the attraction burned itself out? And would it be worth the pain of going back to her solitary life afterwards?

Yes! She opened her eyes again, and brought her chin up. If this was her only chance to experience a little bit of heaven in a man's arms, she would grab it with both hands and make the most of it. Daniel might not love her, but he was honest and he would be straight with her. He was gentle and passionate, touching her body with reverence, making her feel like she was the most desirable woman on earth. She wanted more. She needed more.

So long as she didn't do anything stupid, like tell him how she felt, she might be able to keep him interested. Sitting fretting about how long it would last would simply bring the end closer.

She laughed at her determined expression. *Well, why not? At least she didn't have to worry about him dumping her so that he could marry someone else.* Daniel's aversion to commitment wasn't personal – he didn't want to be tied to any woman.

She could do this. If Robert came through with the new job, she would have at least a month to play her new role as Daniel's lover before she needed to think about what her future held. And she was going to make the most of every chance she had to store up memories for the day when she would inevitably find herself alone again.

Chapter Eight

A few weeks later, Laurel admired her plaster-free wrist and held her first pay-slip in her hand.

She laughed and did a little victory dance around the kitchen. She'd never had so much money before, and the same amount was going to arrive in her bank account at the same time next month, and the one after that. She shook her head in disbelief. They were even setting up a pension for her! Before she'd met Daniel and his friends she'd only dreamed of having the security of a good job and a decent salary. She'd been sleeping in a stock room, for God's sake!

The speed with which her life had changed still made her want to pinch herself. The job that Robert had given her with his charity was demanding but, as he had pointed out, Laurel had the perfect qualifications to enable her to see both what the kids that they aimed to help really needed, and how to approach them with it. Robert had been an absolute sweetheart, talking to her for hours and really listening to what she had to say.

Her induction had been thorough, and Laurel had spent time in every department and visited every project. She'd been concerned at first that, once he'd picked her brains, Robert wouldn't need to keep her on. But he'd seen to it that she'd been put onto the charity's staff development programme, and the Human Resources manager seemed to be booking her onto courses on everything from health and safety to computer skills and even management training over the next few months. She had a future. She had a career!

She was now involved in a major restructuring of the organisation's programmes. The drop-in centres would offer more practical help and advice, as well as the chance to unwind and have some fun; and they were looking at funding some innovative projects to help older teenagers and young adults who had left the care system and hit problems.

She'd learnt that, although Robert provided millions of pounds out of his own fortune, more money was always needed to ensure the effectiveness and sustainability of the organisation's work. A number of people were involved in building support and raising extra funds. In fact, she and Daniel were attending a gala ball at Robert and Pamela's ancestral home that weekend, which they hoped would raise enough money to set up a new building project.

She had been the one to suggest that if young homeless adults could be employed to build low-cost housing units, they would be learning skills, and gaining work experience and qualifications, as well as providing homes for themselves and others. Robert had said it was perfect. The management team had failed to see any flaws in the idea, except that it was going to be expensive. The charity's trustees had agreed that the funds raised from their annual ball – the biggest event in their fundraising calendar, could be allocated to the launching the scheme.

The ball would be attended by hundreds of the great and good, all of them invited with the sole purpose of parting them from their money. She just prayed that Robert's faith in the outcome wasn't misplaced. This particular project had become a passion for her. She knew what it was like to be homeless and without hope. But she was aware that many people had a jaundiced view of 'vagrants and layabouts' which would be hard to overcome.

But what made her more nervous was the fact that this was the first public event that she would attend at Daniel's side. In the weeks they had been together they had kept to themselves. If Daniel had to attend a business function, which he did frequently, he did so alone.

'I don't want to be distracted,' he'd said. 'If you were there I'd be thinking about finding a quiet corner and satisfying my lust. I need to concentrate on business. I'll concentrate on you when I get home.'

She'd been content with that. But she made sure that, when he got home from some tedious function, she gave him good reason to focus his attention on her.

They had few visitors, but as Daniel had predicted, Lucy's father, Gerald Pemberton, had soon made an excuse to call at the house. Her experience with him was enough to put her off repeating the exercise with anyone else.

Laurel really hadn't been keen on the idea of mixing with the people that Daniel did business with. She might have held her own at the dinner party, but she hadn't been comfortable, and she saw no point in getting to know his business acquaintances. After all, he'd made it quite clear their relationship would never progress beyond the physical. She told herself she accepted that, yet she realised that she didn't want to expose herself to the outside world as Daniel French's mistress.

The ball was different though. Laurel's job with the charity gave her a reason to be there in her own right. Even if Daniel hadn't been going, she would have attended, and had already arranged to take a shift helping behind the scenes during the event.

As a friend of Robert, Daniel always purchased enough tickets to fill a table and invited along people who he thought could be persuaded to offer more support to the cause. Although she would be working for a short time, she would eat with Daniel and his guests, and she hoped they might even get the chance to have at least one dance together. She smiled in anticipation. Jo had produced a stunning creation for her to wear, and she couldn't wait for Daniel to see her in it. Nor could she wait for him to take it off her after the ball, when they spent the night at Robert's stately home.

She shook her head and put the precious slip of paper in her bag. It still amazed her how often she thought about being in Daniel's arms. She'd never imagined she would ever feel like this about any man. It worried her that she had become so dependent on him for her happiness. But she refused to worry about that this weekend. This weekend was about the kids – about giving them hope, giving them a chance in life. It gave her so much satisfaction to know that, thanks to her idea and Robert's faith in her vision, there were a group of young people somewhere who would soon have the opportunity to build their own homes. Homelessness meant you had no opportunities, no dreams; only emptiness and despair.

She'd been in that situation herself such a short time ago. She frowned as she acknowledged that she still wasn't so far removed from it in fact.

Although right now she was living at Daniel's house, and sleeping in his bed, she was aware that it wasn't a permanent arrangement. He hadn't said anything, but her natural caution wouldn't allow her to forget it. Every day, she watched for signs that his interest was waning; that it was time for her to go.

But she couldn't regret her decision to embark on an affair with Daniel. Even as she waited patiently for it to end, she revelled in every minute she could spend with him. Her love for him grew with every kiss, every caress, and she greedily stored every moment of happiness away in her memory to sustain her in the future. No man would ever come close to making her feel what Daniel did.

At first she'd been shocked by the depth of his passion. But he had taught her to embrace it along with him. After so many years of guarding herself, it both frightened and thrilled her to learn how easy it was to let go and experience such sensuality. Thanks to Daniel's patient tutoring, Laurel could now rejoice in her womanhood, and he had given her the confidence to know that she could satisfy her man.

For he *was* her man. He might not recognize or want such a title, and Laurel wasn't foolish enough to claim it anywhere but in her heart, but he was hers, just as she belonged to him.

But she was a survivor too. Laurel knew that one day it would end and she would have to walk away, and that would hurt. Oh Lord, it would hurt! But she would survive. Having her own, well-earned cash in the bank helped. At least now she could afford a roof over her head when she needed one. And with any luck, she would be strong enough to go with her pride intact. Daniel need never know how much he meant to her.

In the meantime, Laurel was happy. She refused to let the fears of her old, cynical, untouched self intrude on her idyll. Not yet.

Daniel sat impatiently in the back of a taxi, willing the traffic to part. It had been a long, frustrating day, and all he wanted to do was to get home. He looked at his watch. Six o'clock. Laurel would be there already. When he arrived, she would open her arms and he would walk into them and let her kiss away the stresses of the day. The woman had a remarkable capacity for soothing his workaday tensions away, only to replace them with other, earthier tensions.

It still amazed him how sexually compatible they were. He'd never had a more passionate, willing lover. Laurel matched his desires and increased them with every touch, every look. Sometimes their need for each other was so urgent that they barely made it past the front door before falling on each other in a frenzy of desire. He'd taken her in every room in the house, even on the stairs, when he had simply refused to wait a moment longer before plunging into her willing body. He could feel himself harden just thinking about it.

The taxi moved another few yards and stopped again.

Daniel checked his watch again and wondered whether he should call her.

He was in the act of reaching for his phone before he came to his senses.

Hell! What was he thinking? She wasn't his wife! There was no need to call the little woman to tell her he was held up in traffic, he told himself angrily.

He ran an agitated hand down his face and shook his head as though to clear it. It occurred to him that he'd found himself thinking inappropriate thoughts about Laurel more and more in recent days. The damned woman seemed to be burrowing under his skin, captivating him with her perfect body and willing passion to such an extent that he was beginning to think dangerous, *domestic* thoughts.

It wouldn't do. As tempting and as satisfying as she was, he neither wanted nor needed to be tied to any woman. He'd lived with the consequences of his parents' weaknesses where relationships were concerned, and he wasn't about to make the same mistakes. They had always tried to justify their actions by claiming to be in love. To them, that made it all right to abandon their only child to school or with Florence, or to use him as a weapon to hurt each other. He wanted no part in such a flawed emotion.

What he had with Laurel was much healthier. It was honest. It didn't hurt anyone. She knew the score and didn't ask or expect anything of him other than his passion. Her new job with Robert was a success and she was gaining confidence and independence in leaps and bounds. So long as things stayed that way he would be satisfied. *Wouldn't he? Wouldn't he prefer it if she was a little less independent, a little less detached?*

He frowned, barely noticing the blaring of horns as the traffic around him became completely gridlocked.

For it occurred to him that, even as he told himself he couldn't possibly want more from his relationship with Laurel, he was considering ways to keep her in his house and in his bed, and he got angry whenever he thought about her moving out and moving on with her life without him. That she might then continue that life with another man filled him with rage.

A few minutes later, Laurel answered the phone. Daniel told her crisply he wouldn't be home.

'Something's come up. I've got to go back to work. It could take all evening. Don't wait up.'

'OK. Hope it goes well,' she said before she realised she was talking to a dead line. He'd said what he wanted to say, and hung up.

She shook her head at his abruptness. Most of the time he was charming and well mannered. But occasionally, he seemed to get into a real dog of a mood and turned surly and rude. She knew she shouldn't take it personally, but it always seemed to happen just when they were getting along especially well. One minute she'd be blissfully happy, wondering whether she might have reason to hope that he cared for her after all; but then in the space of a heartbeat she would be painfully reminded of the truth and she would start to wonder whether this was the beginning of the end.

Then she would get angry with herself and with him, and wonder what the heck had happened to the old Laurel, who would have given as good as she got instead of smiling sweetly and taking it all. Loving Daniel was as painful as it was wonderful, and knowing that he didn't return her feelings was beginning to grind her down.

She didn't know how much more of this she could take.

The phone rang at ten o'clock. Laurel picked up the extension in the bedroom.

'Hello?'

'Laurel.'

'Daniel. What's up?'

'Nothing.'

She frowned. So why had he phoned?

'Have you finished your work?'

'Yes.'

'Good. Are you on your way home?'

'I thought I might stay at the office.'

She was silent for a moment. She didn't know what he wanted her to say. Was he starting to distance himself from her, to make her see that his interest was waning?

'Laurel?'

'I'm still here.'

'What are you doing?'

'I'm in bed, reading.'

'Is it a good book?'

'Not particularly. But there was nothing on the TV, and I wasn't sleepy, so …'

'Put the book down.'

'Daniel?'

'Have you put it down?'

'I did as soon as the phone rang.'

'Good. What are you wearing?'

'What's going on?' she asked.

'Tell me what you're wearing,' he demanded in a low voice.

She looked down at the oversize T-shirt covering her body.

'How do you know I'm wearing anything?'

'Because you like to tease me. And I like to strip you. So tell me.'

Laurel smiled. Having Daniel peel away her clothes to reveal her naked skin was a pleasure that they both relished.

'One of your T-shirts. Not very sexy.' But it smelt of him.

'Then take it off.'

'But it's cold,' she pouted. 'And you're not here to warm me up.'

'Take it off, Laurel. I promise to warm you up.'

'How can you if you're still at the office?'

'Do as I say. Take it off. Strip for me.'

Her breath caught in her throat. He sounded so compelling. His deep velvet voice seemed to reach inside her and stir every nerve ending into sensuous delight.

'I'll have to put the phone down.'

'Turn it onto speakerphone.'

'Why?'

'I have plans for you. You'll need both hands free.'

'I'm not into DIY,' she dismissed. 'I like to feel someone else's hands on me.'

There was silence. Laurel waited, her body thrumming.

'Will any hands satisfy you, my little tease?' he asked.

'Oh no,' she breathed. 'Only one very special pair of hands will do. '

'Nothing but the best, eh?'

She could hear the amusement in his voice.

'When you've been taught by a master, then only the very best is good enough,' she agreed.

'So if that special pair of hands were with you now, what would you have them do?'

She laughed softly, and proceeded to tell him in graphic detail, her voice catching in her throat as her body responded to the images in her mind.

'Touch yourself, Laurel,' he urged.

'No,' she denied them both.

'Not even to please me?'

'Oh, I'll please you, Daniel, have no doubt. But if you want me, you have to come and get me.'

The bedroom door opened and he stepped forward. His jacket and tie were gone, the top buttons of his shirt undone, his eyes burning and his skin flushed with the heat of desire. He switched off his phone and tossed it aside before pulling his shirt over his head. He took another step and pulled at his leather belt with trembling fingers. By the time he reached the bed the rest of his clothes had been abandoned

She smiled and rose to kneel on the bed, her arms reaching for him.

'You were saying?' he rasped, pulling her close.

'I can't remember,' she sighed.

'Then let me remind you, my little tease,' he growled. And he did.

Later, when exhaustion had finally claimed Laurel, Daniel lay on his side, studying her in the lamplight. They had made love for hours, urging each other on to ever higher peaks. His body felt heavy and sated. By rights he should be sleeping too. But his mind wouldn't let him rest.

He'd left the taxi earlier and walked back to his office, determined to put some distance between him and the woman who had invaded his home and his mind. He wasn't proud to admit that he'd panicked. For the first time in his life he found himself wanting to break his own rules. He wanted to make sure of her. *To claim her as his.*

He rolled onto his back and laid an arm across his eyes. He couldn't understand it. She was a contrary, feisty little witch, so far removed from the sophisticated, compliant women he'd bedded in the past. He'd expected his unlikely attraction for her to burn itself out quickly; was sure that she'd be long gone by now. But with each day it grew until there were times when all he could think about was touching her, possessing her, hearing her cries as he drove her as crazy with desire as he was.

Any other woman would have bored him before this, or

started to be tiresome and cling.

But Laurel didn't cling, except where he wanted her to – when he was making love to her. The rest of the time she gave him space; didn't demand that she be the centre of his universe; didn't ask anything of him. Not that she let him walk all over her, he conceded. If he acted like a boor, she told him in no uncertain terms. But she didn't sulk either. She was more likely to laugh at him, to tease him out of his ill-humour. He seemed to have laughed more in the past few weeks than he ever had before.

But it wouldn't last. Nothing this intense could be trusted.

Laurel sighed in her sleep. Daniel rolled over to look at her again. He gently brushed a tendril of silken hair out of her face.

She was so beautiful. And her life was suddenly bursting with possibilities. Robert had confirmed what he'd already known. She was bright and determined, and could cut through all the irritating, time-wasting details to pinpoint what was important. Laurel was capable of great things, and she deserved the chance to fly, to show the world how special she was.

But instead of rejoicing that she would move on and leave him to regain the serenity of isolation that he had enjoyed before she crashed into his life, Daniel felt real fear. Just as he had when he'd seen his beloved godmother in mortal danger.

Oh God! I love her!

Even as he shook his head in denial, he knew it to be true. Laurel Park had become as vital to him as breathing.

He lay there for a long time, watching her sleep, until he finally made peace with his feelings for this unexpected, but quite remarkable young woman. And as the dawn light began to soften the darkness outside of the circle of light from her bedside lamp, Daniel slipped into slumber, knowing that whilst he might have to face the possibility that she wanted to be set free, he had to do everything he could to show her that she could fly just as far and as high with him at her side.

The gala ball was held at Robert's country estate. Pamela was acting as her brother's hostess, and had proved to be a dynamo at organising the thousands of details that together made a successful charity event. Laurel had been at the house since mid-morning, as part of a team of staff and volunteers, including Chris and Jo; all of them running to do Pammy's bidding as she ordered them around in a manner that would have made the toughest drill sergeant seem like a marshmallow. She'd even had Daniel snapping to attention a time or two, Laurel recalled with a smile.

But at last the preparations were complete and she had escaped to their allocated room to bathe and change while Daniel stayed behind downstairs to speak to Robert.

Laurel had never expected to be a guest at an honest-to-goodness stately home, and this was the second time she'd been here. The day after his dinner party Daniel had brought her here for lunch. She'd been completely overwhelmed, but he'd just smiled and told her to relax.

'Robert and Pam are good people. Don't let this pile of bricks fool you.'

He'd been right, of course. He'd also made it quite clear to their host that they were now lovers, which had shocked and embarrassed Laurel, even though as she and Daniel were an apparently engaged couple it wasn't a surprise to anyone else. It was all so new to her that she'd barely had time to accept the fact herself, but the way that he touched her and spoke to her had been an exercise in macho possession.

'Did you have to make it so obvious?' she'd asked him on the way home, her cheeks still burning. 'He'll think I'm a right tart!'

'No he won't. He knows I'm very selective.'

'That doesn't make it any less embarrassing,' she complained. 'He's going to be my boss.'

'Exactly.'

'What do you mean by that?'

'Now he knows that you're off limits.' He paused as he negotiated a busy junction. 'I don't share.'

Laurel felt a thrill of excitement at his possessive statement.

'Fair enough,' she'd responded. 'So long as you're clear that I don't either.'

He'd slanted her a crooked smile.

'Fair enough. You'll be too busy with me anyway. I find that your delectable little body has inspired a rather voracious hunger in me, which I intend to satisfy as soon as we get home.'

She wasn't foolish enough to think that was a declaration of any finer feelings. He was simply laying down the ground rules. So long as she didn't stray, and so long as she kept his interest, he would be her lover. As soon as he got bored with her, she'd be out on her ear.

But even knowing that couldn't stop her from almost melting with excitement.

'Well you'd better concentrate on your driving and make sure we get back in one piece,' she'd teased primly.

And his hunger had indeed been voracious that day, and the next, and the next! Laurel felt her cheeks burning as she thought back over the past few weeks. And tonight they would make love in this beautiful room in this amazing house. She ran a hand over the heavy silk covering on the enormous four-poster bed. It was the sort of bed she'd imagined any bride would dream of sleeping in on her wedding night.

Her mind automatically shied away from the thought of weddings. It wasn't going to happen, no matter how much she had begun to yearn for it. Daniel didn't do commitment, and he didn't want marriage or children. She repeated the mantra over and over as she showered in the en-suite bathroom, which she'd been delighted to discover was modern and beautifully equipped.

The trouble was, it was becoming increasing difficult for Laurel to convince herself that Daniel *didn't* care for her. She'd imagined that becoming his mistress would mean that they'd have sex and nothing else. But they enjoyed each other's company both in and out of bed. They talked, they laughed together; and, she acknowledged, their lovemaking seemed to take on a new, deeper dimension as they got to know each other on a non-sexual level.

She shut off the shower and emerged into the steamy bathroom.

As she dried herself she remembered their lovemaking over the past twenty-four hours. She smiled, thinking about how he'd walked into the bedroom, mobile phone to his ear, when she'd thought he'd been miles away at his office. She'd thought herself safe to tease him on the phone, only to discover that her handsome, demanding lover had expected her to deliver on her outrageous fantasies. When he'd finally let her sleep she'd been exhausted, and she'd thought he must be too. But he'd shown no sign of exhaustion this morning when he'd woken her with his lips and his hands. He had been so sweet and tender that she'd cried. Before she'd met Daniel, she'd never cried, especially not happy tears. But then again, she'd never felt so loved and cherished before. It had worried her that Daniel would become irritated by her tears, but he had surprised her again by holding her close and kissing them away, soothing her as though she were the most precious person on earth.

Laurel knew that she was setting herself up for a fall by wanting more from Daniel. But she couldn't help herself. She knew that they were good together, and as her newfound confidence grew she was beginning to think that she deserved more than Daniel insisted he was willing to give. She dared to hope that, despite his ground rules, he was coming to love her too. But if he wasn't, if he didn't change his mind, could she just accept it? Or did she have the strength of will to walk away?

'Not yet,' she whispered. 'Not yet.'

Chapter Nine

'Have I told you how beautiful you look tonight?' Daniel whispered in her ear.

'Yes, but you can tell me again,' she chuckled.

'That shade of green is a perfect match for your eyes, and I love what you've done with your hair.'

He kissed her delicate neck, which had been left exposed by her upswept style, then lifted her left hand to his lips.

'I might just have to buy you some earrings and a necklace to go with this,' he mused as his thumb played with her emerald ring.

'You don't need to do that,' she told him, secretly thrilled.

'I know. But I want to.'

They were seated at a large round table with ten other people, all clients or colleagues of Daniel, including Lucy Pemberton and her father Gerald. Laurel had been dismayed to see the older man. She'd only met him once before, but that was enough. He was an awful man, a bully who expected to get his own way no matter what. It amazed Laurel that Lucy could be so sweet with such a father.

As Daniel had predicted, Lucy's father hadn't accepted their 'engagement' as easily as his daughter, and he'd invited himself to the house to see for himself the woman who had dared to thwart his plans to make Daniel his son-in-law. He'd been charming in a slimy way, raising Laurel's defences immediately. She'd met snakes like him before.

He's shown his true colours when Daniel had left them alone for a moment to find some documents Gerald had asked about.

'I must say I was surprised that Daniel should show such poor judgement, moving a cheap tart into his house. But now that I've seen you I can understand your appeal.'

Laurel had gasped at his attack, wanting to retaliate. But long-honed instincts kept her silent.

'But you can't stay. I have plans for that young man. He'll make an ideal husband for my daughter, and a worthy successor to take over my company in due course. I'm not prepared to let a nobody like you turn his head. Now, I'm prepared to be generous for your co-operation my dear.' He'd named a price that had Laurel gasping again. 'I'll even pay extra for you to leave London and set yourself up somewhere else. But only so long as you leave Daniel for my girl.'

'You can't just buy people!' she'd argued. 'You can't make people fall in love to suit you.'

'You little fool,' he'd laughed. 'Think you're in love with him, do you? Well, don't get your hopes up. I've known him for a long time. The last thing he wants is a love match. That's what I keep telling that stupid daughter of mine. She'll need to toughen up, but she'll learn. A man like Daniel needs a wife who will be an asset to him, increase his power. You might be able to give him sex, but it's obvious you don't have any connections,' he'd sneered, raking her body, clad in cheap jeans and T-shirt, with a contemptuous look. 'You don't stand a chance of keeping him. Men like Daniel don't need to marry tarts like you. You'd be better off accepting my offer and getting out now.'

'And if I don't?'

'Than I will make sure you regret it.'

The venom in his voice even as he smiled had chilled her. With as much dignity as she could muster, Laurel had risen and walked out of the room.

'Think about it, my dear,' his hateful voice had stopped her as she reached the door. 'It's a limited offer.'

She'd told him in the coarsest language she knew where he could shove his offer and fled.

Now she faced him again across the dinner table, and Laurel felt her new found confidence draining away. He had been watching her all through the meal, unnerving her with his loathsome smile whenever she looked up. Daniel had noticed, but shrugged off her unease.

'Forget it. Don't let him get to you. I told you before that his threats are empty. He takes pleasure in upsetting people, especially women. That's why poor Lucy is always trying to please him. He'll never give her his approval because it amuses him to see her suffer. And that's why he tried to get rid of you before. I knew he'd do it. But he still won't get me to marry Lucy. I make my own decisions about who shares my bed.'

Laurel felt her heart shrivel a little more at his words. He hadn't said 'who shares my life', but rather 'who shares my bed'. Nothing had changed.

'Fine,' she said, feeling brittle. 'Just don't leave me alone with that horrible man.'

Daniel smiled and ran a gentle finger down her cheek.

'Now why would I want to leave the side of the most beautiful woman here tonight? You'd be surrounded by crowds of lustful men within seconds.'

'And you don't share, right?'

His grey eyes held her gaze.

'Right.'

He stood up, pulling her with him.

The meal was finished and they were enjoying a short break before the dancing began. There was to be a jazz set for an hour; then an auction hosted by a well-known quiz show host, before the final couple of hours' dancing to a rock band.

'Come on. Let's circulate.'

Laurel gave him a brilliant smile, relieved that he was taking her away from the hateful Gerald.

'OK, but don't let me forget that I've got to go and help with the auction later.'

'There's time to dance first.'

'In these shoes?' she laughed, lifting a foot, her pink-tipped toes peeking out from her delicate silver shoes. It had taken Laurel hours of practice to master the art of walking on the stiletto heels. 'In the words of the late, great Kirsty MacColl, I don't think so.'

She saw desire flare in his eyes as he followed her gaze.

'Don't worry, my sweet tease,' he told her, his deep voice like raw silk on her senses. 'You won't have to move much, just into my arms. I'll keep you from falling.'

Oh Lord! Laurel thought as he gathered her close. *If only he loved me, I could be so totally happy right now.*

'And later on, when we're alone, I'm going to strip every stitch from your delectable body. But I'll leave your shoes on while I make slow, sweet love to you.'

The reminder of her true place in his life killed her silly hopes, even as she felt herself shiver with desire. Trying to act as though he wasn't making verbal love to her in the middle of a crowd of people was a challenge Laurel wasn't sure she was up to. His warm hands caressed her back through the silk of her dress.

'Now who's being a tease,' she laughed softly against his neck, determined that he wouldn't know her heart was breaking.

'You should know by now that I don't tease, my love.'

It was too much. She wasn't his love.

'Don't, Daniel, please!' She couldn't hide the anguish in her voice. 'We both know that you don't do love.'

He stilled, his arms tightening for a brief moment, preventing her from escaping. *Oh God! Why had she said that? He'll be furious!* She closed her eyes to deny the tears that threatened to overspill. She never cried, except for him.

'I did say that, didn't I?' he said softly, his lips gentle against her temple. 'But maybe I'm starting to change my mind. Maybe I'm beginning to think you might be worth the risk.'

Laurel couldn't believe what she was hearing. Did he mean it? Did he really care for her, a nobody whose own mother hadn't thought her worth loving? She leaned back and looked up into his beloved face.

'Is that a problem?' he asked.

In a daze she shook her head.

'Are you sure?' she couldn't prevent herself from asking.

He smiled and kissed her.

She smiled back, her expression one of dazed happiness.

'Absolutely,' he confirmed, before pulling her back into his arms.

Laurel thought she would burst with happiness. She wanted to leap up and down and scream out her joy, but that would mean letting go of Daniel, which she wasn't prepared to do right now. Instead, she contented herself with clinging to him, her wide smile hidden against his neck. With eyes closed, she let him dance her slowly around the ballroom, savouring the joy of being in his arms and in his heart.

A few minutes later she opened her eyes as they turned gently around the dance floor, to look straight into the cold, hateful eyes of Gerald Pemberton. She shivered, feeling his malice reaching out to spoil her happiness. She quickly averted her gaze, but she felt his malevolent gaze following them, like a dark threatening cloud.

I refuse to let him get to me, she told herself. *Daniel loves me and nothing is going to ruin it for us.*

But after a lifetime of having her dreams ripped out of her grasp, a part of Laurel wondered just how long it would be before this dream was torn from her, leaving her heart bleeding and beyond repair. It was so hard for someone with her experience of life to believe that happiness like this could be more than just a dream.

But it is true. My dream has come true. Daniel has rescued me.

With a defiant smile at her tormentor, Laurel snuggled closer to her lover, and turned her back on Lucy's father.

As her line of vision shifted, her attention was drawn to his daughter, dancing close by with a young man who was looking at Lucy with a slightly dazed expression. Laurel smiled. When she saw that the other girl looked equally smitten, she laughed out loud. It looked as though it didn't matter what Gerald Pemberton might have planned for his daughter. Young Lucy was about to break out!

When the jazz session came to an end, Laurel reluctantly left Daniel's side to go and help with the auction. The event team had worked wonders collecting items to be sold, as well as a few things that money couldn't usually buy, such as a round of golf with a champion golfer, a date with a popular actor, and a weekend at a stately home which was even bigger than Robert's pile. It was Laurel's job to record the successful bids and collect payment from the bidders. Business was brisk and she was kept busy. The celebrity host had a line of banter that had the crowd eating out of his hand, and bidding was much higher than they'd hoped.

She worked steadily, concentrating hard because all she wanted to do was think about the bombshell Daniel had dropped on her. He called her his love! She silently urged the host to hurry up so that she could go back to him. She was almost afraid that if she wasn't with him he might change his mind.

'Laurel, do you know where Daniel is?'

She looked up to smile at Sue, Robert's PA.

'I think he said he was going back to our table.'

'Thanks. One of the other trustees wants to introduce him to a potential major donor. As chair of the finance committee, Daniel's the man to answer his questions.'

'Daniel's a trustee?' she asked, appalled.

'Of course. He's been involved since we started,' she confirmed, giving Laurel a quick frown before looking away. 'I didn't realise you ... Oh! There he is! I'd better grab him.'

As she dashed off, Laurel was approached by the latest successful bidder. She smiled vaguely at him, her mind working at full speed, her whole body chilled. If he hadn't told her that he was a trustee of the charity it could only mean one thing – he'd got her this job.

But now wasn't the time to think about it. Even if she was here under totally false pretences, she still had an obligation to fulfil her role tonight. She took a deep breath and concentrated on taking the man's money.

At last, the final bid was knocked down and Laurel was called up on the stage to give the host the total of all the bids. He asked her to read it out. The number was flashed up on a large screen set to one side of the stage and the ballroom erupted with cheers.

'Ladies and gentlemen, thanks to your generosity tonight, we've raised a record amount!'

More cheers and applause filled the room. Even though she was feeling like her whole world was balanced on a knife edge, Laurel made herself laugh and join in the clapping. Just minutes ago, she'd been so thrilled to be a part of all this. Now she didn't know what to think.

She could see Daniel. He was smiling at her with such love and pride. But could she trust what she saw? Was he simply playing with her? She wanted so desperately to believe that he cared, but she knew it was going to be hard to get past the hurt she felt at knowing that he'd not seen fit to tell her about his role with the charity.

She was so wrapped up in her thoughts that she didn't see it coming.

One moment she was smiling at their celebrity host, relieved that she could now slip off the stage and get away for a few minutes to think; but before she could do so the man had taken her hand in his, and she was trapped at his side.

'This is what your generous donations are going towards this evening,' he informed the audience, gesturing towards the screen. As a series of pictures and artist's impressions were shown, he explained the scheme to them.

'And here we have the lovely Laurel Park, the woman whose vision for the self-build programme for disadvantaged youngsters will be realised thanks to your support tonight,' he told them, holding up her hand.

Laurel frowned. She blushed and shook her head as people cheered and whistled. This wasn't supposed to happen. No one had warned her. A quick glance at Robert, standing to one side revealed that he was as surprised as she was. He didn't look particularly thrilled either. Laurel knew that he held great store by the fact that everyone in the organisation was equally valued, from the directors to the office juniors. No one claimed the glory for a campaign or a project for themselves. It just wasn't done.

A movement at the corner of her eye caught her attention. Gerald Pemberton came to stand beside Daniel, triumph stamped all over his face. Laurel was suddenly very afraid. His look told her that he wasn't finished with her yet.

The noise died down and she waited. Lucy's father had done this. He'd set her up. She could feel cold dread seep into every corner of her being. Sadists like Gerald Pemberton never did things by half. There would be more. She knew it, and the host's next words confirmed it.

'Of course, Laurel, you know exactly what it's like to

live on the edge of society, don't you? After all, you're a product of the care system yourself, and have experienced life on the streets. And I understand that, like a number of the charity's beneficiaries, you've even spent some time in prison.'

As he spoke a new image appeared on the screen. A newspaper cutting revealed a picture of a defiant, angry young Laurel in handcuffs, flanked by policemen. The headline read *Charged with attempted murder.*

A ripple of unease ran through the crowd. Someone giggled. For a moment she thought she would faint. Her vision blurred, and nausea rose in her throat. This was far, far worse than she had imagined. She wanted to look at Daniel, but didn't dare. She'd been aware of his shock. No doubt he was regretting his earlier words now that he knew she was a jailbird as well as a nobody.

'Would you like to tell us about it, Laurel?' asked the host with an encouraging smile.

He seemed a long way off as Laurel mentally shrank into herself. In the blink of an eye her old survival skills came into play and she became detached, as though watching the scene from a distance. She looked at the man holding a microphone towards her. He was blithely unaware that he had been used as the instrument of her public humiliation and total destruction.

'I don't think our guests need to hear my pathetic story,' she told him, her voice calm, her expression giving away none of her pain. 'That says it all really,' she waved a limp hand at the screen, wishing they would switch it off. *It was far too sordid and nasty for such a fine, upstanding gathering.*

The host had apparently been led to believe that she was primed to tell her story. She looked him in the eye and gave a tiny shake of her head. He looked non-plussed for a moment before his professionalism took over and he stepped into the dead air and filled the silence.

141

'Well, yes. Er ... It's clear to see that you've put the past behind you, and that you're one of the success stories. And now you're devoting your time to helping others. I think that's wonderful. Yes, quite wonderful.'

He led the bemused crowd in a round of restrained applause.

Laurel wanted to scream. *How the hell can I put the past behind me when you're displaying it on a bloody great screen for the whole world to see?*

Just an hour ago she had been so happy. She had actually touched her hopes and dreams and thought them real. Now she knew that they had been nothing but an illusion. But if she had nothing for herself, she could at least try to do one last thing for the other kids.

She took the microphone from him and faced the audience, her gaze skimming the top of their heads and finally coming to rest on a spot on the back wall. She couldn't bear to look in their eyes. Not yet. Maybe never.

'What you need to know is that, thanks to this organisation, there are young people out there whose lives have been transformed and others who, thanks to your generosity tonight, will have the chance to dream of a home and a future for the first time in their lives.

'It's not easy trying to survive when you've been labelled and dismissed by society. Some survive by getting hard, by fighting back. Others crack under the strain. Few can make it on their own, and without schemes like this and people like Robert and the team who really, really care about what happens to them, they'll be lost.'

Just as I am.

'Thank you all for what you've done tonight, for the money you've given. You have no idea what it means.'

As she turned, she couldn't stop herself from looking at Daniel. He was staring at the screen. The shock and anger on his face tore her frozen heart. But even as it did so, Laurel's pride rebelled. He was judging her. Despite everything they had been to each other over the past few weeks, he didn't trust her. He was seeing just a tiny snippet of the truth and he accepted it and condemned her.

She didn't care what anyone else in the room thought. They didn't know her. They didn't matter. *But Daniel did!*

Damn him! How dare he? And how dare he lie by omission about his involvement in her new job?

They had lived together; she had given him everything – her mind, her body, her soul. The enormity of his betrayals burned, bringing stinging, painful heat coursing through her chilled being.

She handed back the microphone and walked swiftly away. So intent was she on putting as much distance between them as possible, that she didn't even hear the roar of approval and applause that followed her from the ballroom. She'd got as far as the hall before someone stepped in front of her. She would have taken evasive action, but her long dress and high heels caught her out and she stumbled.

Robert stopped her by the simple action of hugging her.

'Laurel, my dear, I'm sorry. I had no idea that was going to happen. I don't know who arranged that. It was a sick joke. But you handled it beautifully. You were magnificent!'

She pushed against him and he released her immediately.

'Are you all right?' he asked. 'You're awfully pale.' When she didn't respond, he led her into a room off the hall and closed the door behind them.

'I'm OK,' she said finally as the noise of the ball receded behind the wooden barrier. *Liar! Not fine, I'll never be fine again. But I'm OK. I'm a survivor. I can do this.*

'Can I get you anything? A brandy, perhaps?'

She shook her head.

'No. Thank you. Look, Robert, I'm sorry about that. Do

you want to sack me, or shall I just resign and save you the bother?'

He looked shocked.

'My dear girl, come and sit down. I have no idea what you're talking about.'

She let him lead her over to a Chesterfield that she remembered sharing with Daniel on their first visit here. She sat, perched on the edge, grasping her hands together on her lap. Robert sat at the other end of the sofa, giving her space.

'You saw it. It's true. I'm an ex-con.'

For a long moment he just looked at her, searching her pale, set face.

'No you're not,' he said eventually, smiling at her.

Laurel frowned. 'I am. I spent three months in Holloway.'

'That's as may be, but you're no criminal, Laurel.'

'Don't be so bloody naïve, Robert!' she cried, jumping to her feet and whirling round to face him. 'You can't just look at someone and decide they're OK! I tried to kill a man! I was locked up because I was a danger to society!'

She had been so wound up by his calm refusal to believe her that she hadn't noticed the door opening. She didn't hear the noise of the rock band playing now in the ballroom, which become muffled as the man who entered closed the door behind him. She didn't see Daniel standing there until she had uttered the damning words.

'So it's true,' he said.

Laurel looked at Daniel's beloved face and saw nothing. No anger, no contempt, no hatred, no love. Just nothing. Whatever he might have felt for her was gone. There was no point in explaining herself. It was too late.

'Yes,' she said, her head held high.

If this was to be the last time he ever looked at her, she refused to let him see her bowed and beaten. She slipped the emerald ring from her finger and offered it to him. 'I'll

144

ask Chris to collect my things,' she told him. 'I'll make sure he leaves the key on the hall table.'

At first he didn't move, didn't react. Laurel wondered whether he'd even heard her. She waited, her arm outstretched, for him to take the ring.

They'd both forgotten about Robert, and they both started slightly when he stood up.

'This is crazy, you two. Laurel, tell him …'

'There's nothing to tell. He knows it all now.'

'No. Daniel, there's …'

'Stop interfering, Robert. This is between Laurel and me.'

'But you're both acting like bloody idiots!' he roared. 'For God's sake, you've got to talk to each other!'

Laurel flinched, but kept her mouth firmly shut. Her pride was all she had left, and if she tried to speak she would end up begging, and then she would have nothing. When Daniel remained silent and unmoving, she carefully placed the ring on a side table and stepped around him. At the door she turned.

'Thank you for everything Robert. I'm going to ou … my room to change now, then I'll get a lift back to town.'

'I brought you here. I'll take you back.' Daniel didn't turn round.

'No. You must stay. You paid for the privilege, after all.'

He did turn at that, his temper finally getting the better of him.

'Oh yes, I've paid, haven't I, Laurel? I paid handsomely to be laughed at! Damn you! Did you enjoy making a fool of me? Letting me believe that I knew you, letting me think I might be able to care? Well, the game's over, you little tease! I thank you for a lesson well taught. I won't be fooled by a woman again. You've reminded me just how treacherous and how creative they are with the truth!'

She stood, her hand on the door handle, letting his anger wash over her. Robert tried to calm him with a hand on his shoulder, but Daniel shrugged him off, pushing him away, his angry eyes never leaving hers.

'Calm down, my friend.'

Laurel thought Daniel was going to hit him, and it must have shown on her face, because all at once he stilled and closed his eyes. Blowing out an agitated breath he ran a hand through his hair before he opened his eyes and looked around him like a man waking from a nightmare. His shoulders slumped and he turned his back on her, as though unable to bear the sight of her.

'I'm sorry, Robert. It's totally unacceptable to act like this in your home. I hope that you'll forgive me. I would hate this to affect our friendship.'

'Of course. Of course.' Robert approached him again and they shook hands.

Laurel allowed herself a small sigh of relief that at least she hadn't been responsible for dividing the friends.

She opened the door and would have slipped out, but Daniel's words stopped her.

'Don't leave on my account,' he told her coldly. 'I'm going. For some reason, the evening has lost its promise.'

He picked up the ring and tossed it at Robert.

'Here. A donation. Put it to some good. I've no use for it.'

Laurel had thought she was beyond pain, but his casual words and action almost brought her to her knees. She barely held it together until he left the room, shutting the door quietly behind him. Then she leaned her back against the door and closed her eyes.

'Laurel?'

'Yes, Robert?' she asked, wishing she were alone, wishing that he hadn't just witnessed the final end to her dreams.

'I know you weren't convicted of anything. Everyone who works for us is subject to police checks. Why didn't you tell him the truth?'

'There's no point. I can't explain now, Robert. But believe me, it's better this way. Daniel didn't trust me. Sooner or later something like this was bound to happen.'

'Would you like that brandy now?' he asked kindly.

She opened her eyes and gave him a sad little smile.

'Yes. I think that would be a very good idea,' she agreed before bursting into tears.

Chapter Ten

Daniel wondered later how he had survived the journey back to London. He had driven away from the ball like a man possessed. He hadn't cared about danger; he was just intent on getting as far away from Laurel as possible.

Damn the woman!

He'd had such high hopes at the beginning of the weekend. For the first time in his life he was in love. He'd truly believed that in Laurel he'd found his soul mate. But she'd made it quite obvious that she didn't feel the same way.

He'd seen Gerald Pemberton when he'd gone back into the hall. The bastard had looked entirely too pleased with himself. He'd stood next to him when Laurel's picture had been flashed on the screen, his soft words confirming that he was the one responsible for putting it there.

'I'm sorry, old chap, but I felt it was important that the truth be known. Can't have criminals like that working with vulnerable children now, can we?'

The urge to punch him then, and again as he approached Daniel as he left the room, had almost been too much. But the first time he'd needed to get to Laurel, and the second time the desire to get away from the whole bloody disaster won out. He would deal with Gerald another day, when he was capable of rational thought. One thing was sure – he would have nothing more to do with the man, either personally or professionally. With Daniel's reputation in the business world, his actions would be noted and Pemberton would suffer.

Young Lucy had run up to him as he'd headed for the

door. She'd grabbed his sleeve and held on when he would have ignored her.

'Daniel! Is Laurel all right?'

'Oh, she's just dandy,' he'd drawled, his temper barely under control.

'I can't believe my father did that!'

'How do you know it was him?'

'Because he just told me. He said he'd made sure the field was open for me. But Daniel, I didn't want this! I like Laurel. And to be honest, I don't think I really wanted to be your girlfriend at all. You're far too ... you know ...'

'I get the message,' he told her harshly. *Dear God, was he so bloody awful that every woman in his life was there under false pretences? Did every damned female have to be coerced into a relationship with him?* 'You pursued me to gain your father's approval. Isn't it about time you started living for yourself instead of letting him treat you like a chattel to be sold to the highest bidder?'

Lucy looked stricken, but kept it together when he thought she would burst into tears. Her brave dignity in the face of his angry hostility reminded him of Laurel. *Damn her!*

'You're right, Daniel. I'm never going to gain his approval just for being who I am, am I?'

'After what he's just done to Laurel, do you honestly believe his approval is worth anything?'

'Maybe not. But because he's my father, it's been hard to accept. I think tonight the time has come for me to grow up and face the truth.' She took a deep breath and took a step back, releasing him. 'I'm sorrier than you'll ever know that my naivety led to this. Please tell Laurel. I don't believe any of it, and if I'd known what he had planned I'd have warned you.'

He hadn't stayed long enough to tell her that he wouldn't be telling Laurel anything – that she'd rejected him. Instead, he simply left her standing there.

Now he sat slumped in his car outside his house. He looked at the façade, cold and aloof in the predawn, the harsh light from the street lights casting stark shadows. When he'd left there less than twenty-four hours ago with Laurel he had been a happy man. Going back in there now, alone, knowing that she wasn't coming back was something he didn't have the will to do.

Daniel restarted the engine. He couldn't go in there, and he knew he wouldn't sleep. So he might as well go to the office. His work was the only thing in his life he could be sure of. From now on he would concentrate on that. He would work Laurel Park out of his system, and he would never again make the mistake of trusting a woman with his heart.

Within twenty-four hours, Daniel left the country on an extended business trip. He would visit his interests in New York, Chicago, Hong Kong, and Singapore.

Laurel had lived through bad times before. When she'd been locked in a prison cell for twenty-three hours a day for three months on remand she'd thought that nothing could ever be worse. But she was wrong. She could walk around freely now, could do whatever she wanted, except what mattered most. She couldn't be with Daniel. She was locked in the prison of her own misery.

She'd been unable to make any decisions for herself in the hours that followed Daniel's departure from the ball, so Robert and Pamela had taken over. They'd protected her from the crowds, secreting her away until the last guests had left or retired to bed. It had been an ordeal returning to the room she'd shared with Daniel. He'd left without stopping to collect anything but his wallet and car keys. With shaking hands she'd gathered up his clothes and toiletries and carefully folded them into this overnight bag. Robert agreed to return it to him.

Unable to stay, Laurel wanted to go back to London

with Chris and Jo, but learned that they'd already gone. Instead, Pamela had stepped in, ignoring her protests when she'd taken Laurel to her own flat in Knightsbridge.

'Don't be silly. You need somewhere to stay and I've got heaps of room. You can stay as long as you like. I'd appreciate the company, and it's handy for your office.'

'But I quit.'

Pamela shook her head.

'Robert won't accept your resignation. They need you, and when you've had time to calm down and think about it, you need the job, Laurel.'

'But I don't think I can do it. Not now,' she whispered.

'If you're worried about what that bloody Pemberton man did, you shouldn't. Robert intends to make sure that everyone at the ball knows the truth.'

'The truth is I went to jail.'

Laurel had been touched by Robert and Pamela's sincere distress over what happened, both at the ball and between her and Daniel. Shamed by their concern, she told them the truth about both her incarceration and her fake relationship with Daniel.

'You were on remand. Like hundreds of others who are denied bail because they don't have a home. Don't you see? It's still happening. Even though most of them are eventually acquitted, too many youngsters are locked up and brutalised by the penal system. We need to sort it out. You've got to stay and help us.'

'I honestly don't think I can,' Laurel replied. 'I ... can't think about it now.' *Not when all I can think about is Daniel's face as he left me.*

'It's all right, my friend. You don't have to make any decisions right now. It's obvious that you're dead on your feet. Come on, I'll show you where you can sleep.'

Late the next day Robert arrived with her things. She wanted to ask about Daniel, but didn't have the courage. She had hardly slept a wink, missing him, trying to come to terms with the fact that from now on she would sleep alone. It was funny how after such a short time she had grown accustomed to sharing a bed with him.

In the end, Robert told her anyway.

'I couldn't get away until the last guests had left this morning. I tracked him down at his office. He was still in his dinner suit. I don't think he'd even been home. He's burying his head in business so that he doesn't have to face up to his feelings.'

'I told you, he has no real feelings for me. It was all a charade.'

'But he loves you, Laurel,' Robert insisted. 'I've known him most of my life, and he's never been as happy as he has been in the past few weeks with you.'

She shook her head, refusing to believe him no matter how much she wanted it to be true.

'It was all a lie,' she insisted. 'He was playing a part.'

'Rubbish!' argued Pamela. 'He might have a poker face for business, but believe me, Daniel French has never been that much of an actor. No, he cares. If he didn't he wouldn't have made such an ass of himself.'

'It doesn't matter. It's over now.'

'Won't you at least try to explain ...?'

'No.' She had too much pride for that. If he was so willing to think badly of her, then he didn't deserve an explanation. 'There's no point. Daniel and I never had a future together. I wasn't even supposed to be staying at his house for more than a few days. It's time for me to move on.'

She hesitated before turning to her boss.

'I know I said I'd resign, Robert. But I'd appreciate it if I could stay until I find another job.'

The money she had in the bank now wouldn't last long, and she wouldn't be able to find any decent accommodation without a regular income. Resigning from a perfectly good job would mean that she'd be refused unemployment benefit. And if living with Daniel had taught her anything, it was that she deserved better than to sink back into her old life on the edges of society.

'I told you at the time I wouldn't accept your resignation,' he assured her. 'So that's no problem. I want you to stay anyway. You're made for the job, Laurel.'

'But ...'

'No buts. What Gerald Pemberton did at the ball was rotten, and he's taking plenty of flack for it. A lot of people have contacted me to say how impressed they were by how you handled the whole thing.'

While Pamela had looked after the distraught Laurel, Robert had sprung into action. Gerald had been told to leave. In her first act of rebellion Lucy had refused to go with him, choosing instead to accept a lift from a friend. By the time everyone else began to leave Robert had prepared a statement to be handed to each of them. It declared that, like all staff and volunteers working for the charity, Laurel had been subject to a police check which confirmed that she had never been convicted of any crime. It went on to say that the organisers wished it to be known that they had not authorized this malicious breach of her privacy, and they would fully support her in any action she decided to take against the person or persons responsible.

When she read that she actually laughed. The thought of suing Gerald Pemberton for defamation was tempting, if only to annoy the man. But she was realistic enough to know that he had the money to employ a team of high-powered lawyers to ensure his eventual victory. After all, she couldn't deny that the press article had been genuine. She *had* been arrested for attempted murder. The fact that the charges were later dropped didn't render the basic facts untrue.

'You mustn't give him another victory, Laurel. If you leave your job you've let him have it all. The best revenge is to live well. '

'I know,' she sighed. 'But until the ball I hadn't even been aware that Daniel was a trustee. How can I carry on working there in the circumstances?'

'I did wonder why he hadn't told you, but he said you'd assume he'd pulled strings to get you the job.'

'Didn't he?' she asked bitterly.

'Other than inviting me to dinner and manoeuvring you into talking, no. He simply set up the situation and left us to it.'

That sounded like Daniel. He was a master of the fine art of manipulation. *Damn him!*

'But whether he's a trustee or not is irrelevant. You never came across him at the office before, did you? I'd say it's unlikely you will in the future.'

'How do you know he won't insist on you sacking me?'

'He won't do that, Laurel. You know him better than that,' he chided. 'And I hope you know me better than that too. I would never let friendship take precedence over the best interests of the charity, and if by some unlikely chance Daniel should try it, then it would put a severe strain on our relationship.'

Once again Laurel felt herself burn with shame.

'I'm sorry, Robert. You're right. I should have known better.'

He smiled. 'Don't worry about it.'

'And don't worry about finding somewhere to live,' said Pamela. 'I'm fed up with living on my own. If you stay with me you'll be saving me from surrendering to spinsterhood and buying myself a cat.' She shuddered dramatically. 'I hate the creatures.'

They all laughed. Again, Laurel was amazed that she could. She realised that although she might never feel truly happy again, she would survive.

In fact, she wondered whether she had really been happy before, even when everything had seemed so wonderful with Daniel.

No, I wasn't, she conceded. *I was simply waiting for something like this to happen. I never expected it to last.* It didn't make it hurt any less when the worst had happened though.

And so Laurel moved into one of Pamela's spare bedrooms and carried on working for Robert at the charity. Everyone treated her with kindness and respect, and she worked hard, filling her days so that she didn't have time to think about how much she was missing Daniel. Robert had brought her the news that he had gone abroad on business, and she told herself that she was relieved because she wasn't in danger of meeting him for the next few weeks.

She lost weight. The few pounds that she had to spare on her slender frame seemed to fall away, leaving her looking like a wraith. But if her friends voiced their concern she would smile and change the subject. She was all right. She would survive. She just needed a little more time to get used to being without him.

But at night she lay, dry-eyed and sleepless. Even as she told herself that he'd never really been hers, she knew that he was her heart, her soul. Daniel was her one true love, the only man she wanted.

She wondered whether she should have tried to explain to him, or even if she should have told him everything at the beginning. But he'd been so suspicious of her at first that to reveal she'd been in prison would have been foolish in the extreme, no matter that she'd been innocent. At the ball they'd both been so angry. She had been furious that he had taken one look at the picture and headline and believed it. The fact that she'd suspected he'd fixed her job had also fueled her pride and temper.

With the benefit of hindsight, she realised that there was no reason for him to doubt what he'd seen. It had been utterly damning. But it had hurt her so much that, after living together, after she'd given herself to him and him alone, he hadn't questioned what he'd seen. Instead he had simply accepted that she was capable of such a thing and rejected her.

In the cold light of another dawn, two long weeks after the ball, Laurel finally accepted that if she was ever going to be able to move on with her life, she needed to face Daniel and at least try to explain everything to him. It wouldn't make any difference to how he felt, but she needed to make her peace with him.

If a tiny part of her nurtured the hope that he might truly love her, Laurel forced herself to ignore it. It wasn't going to happen. She needed to accept that. And maybe facing him was the only way she could do so.

When he returned to London she would go and see him.

Putting oceans and continents between himself and Laurel did Daniel no good at all. He still couldn't forget her. He'd buried himself in work, punishing himself with sixteen-hour days, only to lie sleepless night after night. Even as he told himself he was a fool, he went over everything that had happened between them from the moment they'd been introduced at the restaurant.

He couldn't believe that he'd got it so wrong. Even when he'd seen the damning evidence displayed for all the world to see on a twelve-foot screen, he hadn't been able to believe it. He'd gone to find her, expecting her to explain, but she'd shut him out, denying nothing. She hadn't tried to justify it, or defend herself. She'd simply looked at him with furious pride and taken off his ring.

Robert had tried to tell him that there was more to the story than Pemberton had revealed, but at the time he hadn't been prepared to hear it. He'd since searched the internet and found a copy of the article. He knew the things that had been written about Laurel in the paper – speculation that she might have been a prostitute, for example – were absolutely untrue, but he'd been in no mood to hear any more about it then. The fact that Robert knew more about it than he did had enraged him.

But now, after two weeks of misery, Daniel was ready to listen. It hadn't taken him that long to realise if the press had got something so fundamental wrong, then they were probably wrong about everything else. As he prepared for his flight home, he acknowledged that if he was to move on he needed to see Laurel and find out if there was even the slightest chance that they might resolve this.

He put through a call to Robert, and after a long conversation confirmed that he was coming home. He hoped his friend took the hint and passed the information on to the person he really wanted to know.

From the moment Robert told her when Daniel was due home Laurel's foolish heart had been battling with her more practical mind. Did she dare hope? Had he been as miserable without her as she had been without him? She'd tried to stop herself from allowing her heart to believe that there might still be a chance for a fairytale ending for them. She knew better than that. She had to be strong and accept that it was over.

She just needed to see him, to explain the things she'd refused to reveal to him before, to apologise. He deserved that at least. He had done so much for her. She'd even come to terms with his interference in securing her job. But Daniel was a proud man and she'd hurt him. His sense of fairness would ensure that he would accept her apology, but she shouldn't expect that all would be forgotten. Much as she wanted to, she couldn't expect him to want her back in his life.

So here she was, standing in the shadows under the trees opposite Daniel's house, waiting for him to come home. She leaned against the park railings, staring across the street with longing. It would have been nice to have gone in and waited for him in the warm. She missed her favourite spot in his study, where she'd curl up in the big leather chair and wait for him to come home in the evenings. But she had no right to enter Daniel's home uninvited.

She heard the chiming of the hour from the bells of the church around the corner. It was late. Daniel would be tired. Maybe she should wait a day or so, and give him a chance to rest? Even as she formed the thought she knew she couldn't do that. She had to see him. She had to know.

The low diesel rumble of a black cab turning into the square had Laurel pressing herself flat against the railings, even though the sight of her would have been obscured by the cars parked at the kerb in front of her. The taxi stopped outside Daniel's house. When Laurel realised she was holding her breath, she let it out on a nervous giggle, so relieved was she that he was home at last.

When Daniel emerged from the vehicle Laurel began to move, only to halt almost immediately as he turned and reached into the cab, helping a young woman to alight. Laurel watched in horror as the other passenger stumbled slightly and was caught in Daniel's arms. She closed her eyes, but was unable to block out the sound of their laughter. She must have made a sound, because suddenly Daniel looked round. Laurel shrank down, hiding behind a car. She couldn't bear to be discovered watching her former lover with his new girlfriend like some obsessed stalker.

She stayed where she was, crouching on the pavement, trembling in fear of discovery, until she heard Daniel open the front door. She heard him talking to the cabbie, who was carrying their bags in. She stood up cautiously and saw all three of them disappear into the house, and then the light going on in the drawing room. For a few seconds Daniel was silhouetted in the front window.

Laurel remembered the dream she'd had weeks before,

when she'd first arrived at the house. Then as now, she had stood outside in the cold and dark, watching him in the light and warmth, wishing she could be part of that light and warmth, part of his life. As in her dream, he now looked out into the darkness, as though aware of her presence. Laurel knew he couldn't possibly see her in the dark, but she felt held captive by his gaze anyway, as though he could see into her very soul. His grim expression matched his image in her dream.

She wanted to walk away, but she knew she had to wait. It wasn't over yet.

Sure enough, a moment later his companion came into view. She was a pretty young woman with short, dark hair. She laid a hand on his shoulder and reached up to kiss him on the cheek.

Laurel didn't need to see any more. She remembered how this dream ended. Before he could turn his back on her, Laurel was moving, running swiftly away.

Chapter Eleven

Eventually she slowed to a walk, her heart and mind as numb with cold as her body. She had her answer. He'd found someone else already. He didn't care after all.

With no direction in mind, Laurel kept walking. So now she knew. He probably hadn't cared much at all, given the speed with which he'd replaced her. She should have known better than to believe that a man like Daniel French would think twice about the likes of her. She was only glad she'd seen how it was for herself. Now she could forget him and get on with her life. He would never know how close she had come to making a fool of herself and begging him for another chance. If he ever saw her again, he would never know that he'd broken her heart.

She would do what she'd intended to do before she met Daniel French – work hard at her career and make a good life for herself. If that life now seemed hollow and painfully lonely, then so be it. It was safer than putting herself through hell again for the sake of a foolish dream of being rescued and living happily ever after.

Cold and exhaustion finally got the better of her, and Laurel headed for Pamela's flat. She let herself in quietly, not wanting to disturb her friend. The last thing she needed right now was to face Pamela's well-meaning questions.

She needn't have worried. The place was in darkness. Without bothering with the lights, Laurel walked into the living room and sank down on the sofa. She was so tired. She really ought to just go to bed. But Laurel couldn't face it. She still hadn't managed to reconcile herself to sleeping alone, hated waking up to the stark reality that the only time she would ever touch Daniel now was in her dreams.

She sighed and laid her head back. She couldn't be bothered to move. She closed her eyes and waited for oblivion take her.

'Hello, Laurel.'

Her breath caught in her throat. For a moment there she could have sworn she heard his voice. She shook her head, refusing to open her eyes.

He can't possibly be here. He's at home with his new lover.

Laurel relaxed as she realised she must be asleep. *He always comes to me when I sleep, when my defences are down.*

'Go away. Can't I even dream in peace?'

'Are you dreaming of me, my darling?'

'Always. It's my punishment.'

'For what?'

'For loving you.'

'If you love me then why did you leave me?'

'I didn't. You left me.'

'You left me tonight. I saw you. Why?'

'You brought another woman home. I saw her.'

'You thought I'd replaced you already?'

'I saw her. You didn't love me. I was just another charity case for you.'

'You mustn't believe everything you see, my love. You should know that.'

She gave a little sob, shaking her head.

'But there's always just enough of the truth to make it damning, so no one will believe you.'

'You won't know until you face it. Tell me your truth Laurel. I want … I need to know.'

'What's the point? You're not really here. You're a dream. I escaped you in real life, but you keep invading my dreams. Why won't you let me be?'

'I'm not a dream, Laurel, open your eyes.'

'No. Please don't make me.'

'Why not?'

'Because even though it hurts, I can't bear to lose this last link with you,' she whispered, her voice thick with tears. 'Even when I'm telling you to go away, I need to keep this little part of you. Let me keep my dreams of you at least.'

She felt the air stir, heard the click of a light switch. Behind her eyelids she became aware that someone had turned on a lamp.

'Open your eyes, Laurel,' he commanded softly.

With a sigh, she obeyed him, expecting to find Pamela standing over her as she broke her fragile link with her dream. But it was Daniel's beloved face that filled her vision. With a soft cry she reached out and touched his cheek. He smiled and covered her trembling hand with his own, before turning to place a kiss against her palm.

Laurel blinked away tears, not wanting anything to mar the sight of him. How was this possible?

'How …?'

'I saw you. You didn't think I'd let you get away again, did you?' he smiled.

He had been kneeling in front of her, but now he moved to sit beside her. As he did so Laurel remembered that he'd been with another woman. Before he realised her intention, she levered herself up and away from him.

'You've got a bloody nerve!' she accused him. 'Did you leave her waiting in your bed? Does she know you're here?'

With a growl of frustration, Daniel sat forward, his forearms resting on his thighs as he pinned her with an irritated look.

'I should have guessed you'd become difficult the moment you realised you weren't dreaming,' he grumbled. 'But for your information, there is no one in my bed, and if the *she* you're referring to is the woman I shared the taxi

163

with, then yes, she does know I'm here. I'd spent the entire flight telling her about how I was coming home to win you back; and she's now right where she wants to be – in her own home in the arms of her husband.'

'But I saw you together! She practically threw herself into your arms, and you took her into the house.'

He shook his head.

'She tripped getting out of the taxi. She needed to go to the toilet and couldn't wait until she got home,' he explained. 'If you'd have stayed round long enough you'd have seen her come out again and leave in the taxi. Alone.'

Laurel didn't know what to say. Could it really have been that innocent? Had she misjudged him? But even if she had, did it really make any difference? Hadn't she just spent the last few hours walking the streets of London reminding herself of all the reasons why she needed to forget Daniel French?

'So,' his deep velvet voice broke into her thoughts. 'Now that we've cleared that up, can we talk about how much you love me?'

Oh dear God!

'No! I don't love you,' she denied.

He smiled and sat back, resting his arms along the back of the sofa and hooking one foot across the other knee. It annoyed Laurel that he could look so damned relaxed when she was a bundle of screaming nerves.

'Yes you do. You just told me.'

'I was asleep.'

He shook his head. 'No, you weren't.'

'Well, I thought I was. And how did you get in here anyway?' she demanded, clutching at any chance to distract him.

This was too humiliating. Did he intend to take everything, even her pride? Surely he would take pity on her and leave her with some dignity?

'You'd disappeared by the time I got rid of my

164

temporary guest and could follow you. I knew you were staying here so I rang Pammy and asked her to help me. She let me in to wait for you. She's not here, by the way. She very kindly offered to spend the night at a hotel. At my expense of course,' he smiled wryly. 'She thinks you should give me a chance.'

A chance for what? To break her heart again?

Laurel took a step back, one hand raised as if to ward him off.

'No,' she said, shaking her head. 'No chance. There's no point.'

Daniel stood up and walked towards her. Laurel backed away until she came up against Pamela's bookcase. He kept on coming, trapping her by placing his hands on the shelves on either side of her.

'Of course there's a point. I love you.'

'Stop it!' she shouted, taking refuge in her temper. 'You don't do love, or commitment! And why would you love a nobody like me anyway? I'm sick of being a bloody charity case!'

'Then stop acting like one,' he countered, his own anger rising.

'I'm not … I …'

'Oh yes, you are,' he accused. 'You're so wrapped up in how hard done by you are, you refuse to give yourself credit for who you are and what you've achieved. You're a coward, Laurel Park! You refuse to accept that I can love you and be proud of you because then you'd have to take the risk and admit that you love me too!'

He twisted away from her, and immediately Laurel wanted to cry out and bring him back. But what would be the point? *It's better like this,* she told herself as she watched him move to the other side of the room.

'You say you're proud of me, Daniel. Well then you're a fool. I'm nothing to be proud of. I'm a jailbird. Just like old man Pemberton told you. I spent three months banged up in Holloway. After a stretch there you never lose the stench. It follows you no matter how far or how fast you move.'

'I read what they said in the papers,' he confirmed. 'But as we agreed earlier, things aren't always what they seem, are they? I know for a fact that you weren't a prostitute.'

She shot him an angry look. *Of course he knew that! He was the only one that did for sure, though.*

'So why don't you stop being a coward and tell me the truth, Laurel?'

'I just did. I'm a criminal. End of story. Now just leave.'

She didn't know how much more of this she could take. Even as she formed the thought she realised that it was ridiculous, given that she had gone to his house tonight to tell him everything.

He leant against the wall and crossed his arms over his chest. He was going nowhere.

'You're no criminal,' he said, no trace of doubt in his voice.

Laurel laughed, a touch of hysteria creeping in.

'Don't kid yourself! I'm definitely one of society's undesirables. I almost killed a man.'

'What did he do to you?'

His quiet words gave her pause. She saw one corner of his beautiful mouth quirk up as he registered the hit.

'Nothing,' she denied, unwilling to look him in the eye.

He pushed away from the wall and began to move towards her.

'I don't believe you.'

Laurel felt panic rise. *He mustn't come close. I can't fight him when he touches me!*

'You'd better believe it,' she told him, aggression twisting her features. 'I attacked him! You'd better watch out, Posh Boy, I'm dangerous!'

He shook his head, laughing.

'Posh Boy? Come on, Laurel, you can do better than that!'

He stood in front of her again and reached out to frame her face in his hands. Laurel's eyes were huge as he pulled her gently towards him and gave her a brief kiss. She closed her eyes and sighed. Daniel tilted her head and kissed her forehead, then gathered her close. She rested her head on his shoulder in surrender. She couldn't fight this anymore.

'You only attack in self defence,' he told her, his voice vibrating through his chest, surrounding her. 'And you'd lay your life on the line for others. If he didn't touch you, then you were rescuing someone else.'

'How did you –?' she looked up at him, amazed that he'd worked it out.

'I know you. So trust me and tell me.'

'It's not pretty,' she warned him, her eyes bleak with remembered pain.

'But it's over. Tell me, Laurel, so that we can put it behind us and move on.'

'OK,' she agreed, resting her cheek against his chest. 'But keep holding me. Please.'

'Of course.'

Her arms crept round his waist, as though she didn't quite trust him to stay there. He smiled and kissed her hair.

'I'm not going anywhere, Laurel,' he assured her.

She was silent for a long moment, gathering her courage. She'd never talked about it, had refused to think about it since the day she walked out of prison. But Daniel was right. She needed to face it so that she could move on.

'I was sixteen. I'd finished my last GCSE exam and was supposed to be moving into my own little flat the next week, and I'd been interviewed for a job as a trainee cashier at a bank. They were going to send me to college on day-release. I thought the world was great and I had so

167

much hope for the future. I was escaping from Social Services and the stigma of being in care. I reckoned I could do anything.

'I was in the park, just enjoying the sunshine on my face and the feel of the grass under my feet, when I heard someone scream. I ran towards the sound and saw a man assaulting a young boy. He ...' She shook her head. 'Anyway, I grabbed a stick – a big one – and started beating the guy off. He had to let go of the boy, and he turned on me. I knew he'd kill me for sure,' she shuddered. 'He was big. And furious.'

Daniel ran a soothing hand over her back, holding her closer.

'Go on.'

'I swung the stick and caught him on his privates.'

'Ouch!' Daniel laughed. 'Good for you!'

'Yeah, well, he shouldn't have been waving them about in a public place,' she gave a mirthless chuckle. 'Anyway, it knocked him off his feet. He went crazy, cursing and screaming, threatening all sorts of foul, disgusting stuff. He said I hadn't saved the boy, only put off the inevitable. He knew where the boy lived, and he could get to him any time he wanted. The kid just stood there and cried. He told me he lived in a children's home and this guy had some sort of authority over it. I just lost it. He should have been protecting the kid, not abusing him. I swung the stick at his head, knocked him out cold, and kept on swinging until someone pulled me off him.'

Daniel went to speak, but Laurel stopped him.

'No, let me finish this. Just hold me and listen, OK?'

'OK,' he agreed, his voice husky with repressed emotions.

He stroked her hair, and she snuggled closer.

'The boy disappeared. He'd been totally freaked out by the guy's assault and his threats. He just took to the streets and never went back to the home. Without him, I had no

168

one to back me up. All the witnesses could remember seeing was me hitting the guy. When he regained consciousness he claimed I'd propositioned him and when he'd refused I'd attacked him. He was a fine, upstanding member of the community. My social worker reported that I had a temper and had used violence before. There was no question in anyone's mind who to believe.'

'Hang on,' Daniel interrupted. 'You've got a temper, yes, but you're not violent.'

'Not without cause, no. I gave as good as I got, that's all. One foster family took in kids and spent the money they got from social services on their own lad – a boy called Damian. He was well named – the evil little sh ... Anyway, his favourite game was to inflict pain. When he broke my wrist, I retaliated and broke his nose. He said I started it and they believed him. I got a reputation for violence.'

Dear God! Had no one helped her? Daniel had had no idea how much she had suffered.

'Go on.'

He felt her shrug.

'You saw the newspaper. They put me on remand pending trial. I'd have been convicted and still there now, but the guy got overconfident and was caught on CCTV assaulting another boy. When the news came out the boy I'd saved came forward and others followed. The guy got twelve years. I could still have been tried, but the powers that be decided to release me. I was stupid enough to think I could pick up where I left off, but life's not like that. Like I said, the stench sticks. I ended up on the streets for a while, fighting for every step forward.'

'How did you cope?'

She shrugged. 'You just do. You cope or you die. I've done whatever I've had to do, and until that lorry wrecked the restaurant I was doing OK.' She laughed. 'Maybe not by your standards perhaps, but I'd been supporting myself and I'd finally managed to get my A-levels. I wasn't intending to spend the rest of my life sleeping on a floor and working as a waitress.'

She was silent for a while. 'Actually, I suppose the accident wasn't such a bad thing. I know I kicked up, but you did me a favour. A lot of favours, in fact. I would never have met Robert and been able to get the job I have now without your help. I just hated that I couldn't do it on my own.

'You'd have done it, Laurel. I have no doubts.'

'Yeah, I probably would have.' She gave him a tired smile. 'It would have taken me a decade or two longer without your help. But I was getting there. I honestly thought I was doing OK when I met you. Then less than an hour after you walked in the door, bam! My whole world literally fell down around my ears. If you hadn't rescued me I'd be back on the streets.'

'Does that mean you forgive me?' he asked, stroking her cheek.

She studied his face, a worried frown on her pale face. He'd been right. Talking had helped. But it had also put a lot of things into their proper perspective.

'I suppose so,' she said eventually.

'Good.' He gave her a swift kiss on the lips, then bent to nuzzle her neck. 'God, I've missed you! I couldn't bear the thought of going home without you.'

Laurel couldn't help it. She reared back as though she'd been stung.

'Home? You want me to move back in with you?'

'Of course. We're meant to be together, Laurel. You know it as well as I do.' He frowned. 'But I can see from your face that you're not ready to accept that, are you?'

Laurel took a deep breath. She didn't know what was wrong with her. She loved Daniel, would love no other person on this earth in the same way. Of course she wanted to move back into his house, into his bed.

'But?' he prompted, reading her thoughts, uncertainty making him impatient. 'Come on, Laurel, spit it out. What possible objection can you have to coming back to me?'

She could feel his tension. Or was it hers? Laurel wished she could soothe them both, but she didn't know how. She struggled to find the words to explain what she was feeling. It was so hard to think straight when he was so close. She pushed against him, half expecting him to refuse to relinquish his hold on her. But he did, and she stepped away and began pacing, not knowing what to do now that he'd set her free.

'I don't know what you're asking of me,' she whispered eventually.

'Don't you?'

She stopped and searched his face.

'You want us to go back – to how we were?'

'Is that what you want?' he countered.

'You're not going to help me on this, are you?' she accused, hands on hips.

'You're not the only one with any pride, Laurel.'

'Huh! That's a joke, right? Correct me if I'm wrong, but I'm the only one who's just had her whole sordid, pathetic life opened up for scrutiny here!'

He looked startled.

'You want my life story? Is that it?'

She blew out an exasperated breath.

'It might help! You never talk about your childhood or your family. What little I know I've heard from Florence or Robert and Pammy. And it's pretty clear that you've kept them in the dark about most of it too. Why should I have to tell you all my deepest, darkest secrets if your life is a closed book?'

'Is that all?'

She shrugged. 'It's a start.'

He laughed. A full-bodied belly laugh. Laurel stared at him aghast.

'I'm trying to make an important point here, Daniel French, and all you can do is laugh?'

'Come here, you adorable woman!' he ordered, reaching for her. 'Are you going get cross every time I'm happy?'

'What have you got to be happy about? Ooh, you are seriously annoying me,' she warned, evading his hands and putting the sofa between them. 'If the thought of telling me about your childhood is so laughable, maybe you'd better just leave!'

'Not on your life,' he told her. 'I'm in for the duration. I can't guarantee I won't make you angry again either. Every relationship has its ups and downs, after all.'

'You patronizing so-and-so! We don't have a relationship! Haven't you heard a word I've said?'

He was still smiling, much to her irritation.

'I heard everything, Laurel, and if it makes you happy I'll tell you everything you want to know as well.'

'You will?' She blinked in surprise.

'I will.' He touched her cheek. 'But not tonight, my love. I think we've had enough heartache for one night.'

'But you will?'

He nodded, his grey eyes shining as he leaned down and kissed her.

She couldn't believe he'd agreed so readily. She'd expected him to kick and fight against it. *Oh Lord! She couldn't think when he kissed her like that!* She pushed him away again.

'Stop that! I haven't finished.'

'There's more?'

Why on earth did that make him look even more pleased with himself? He was confusing her, driving her crazy with frustration. The urge to give in and leap on him and kiss him senseless was starting to look like a good option, but Laurel knew she had to set some ground rules now, or she would never feel secure in their relationship.

'Yes. Now sit down, Daniel, before you run out of favours. You are seriously annoying me at the moment.'

A strong man trying to look meek just doesn't work. She scowled at him, crossing her arms to stop herself from reaching over to try and throttle him. *Who said she wasn't the violent type? And how had the most important conversation of her life taken on an element of farce?*

'Are you winding me up, Daniel?' she demanded.

It would make sense of his strange reactions, of his mirth. He had come here to humiliate her. To take sick revenge.

He sat, seemingly relaxed, an enigmatic smile on his face as he looked up at her.

She looked magnificent in her agitation. Her colour was high, her chest heaving as she fought for control with deep, angry breaths.

'Not at all, my love,' he assured her. 'But maybe I'm being a bit premature in celebrating my happiness.'

'You're happy that you're annoying me?' she asked, her eyes narrowing dangerously.

He laughed again. 'Not exactly. I'm happy because you love me.'

She opened her mouth to protest, but he held up a hand to stop her.

'If you didn't, you wouldn't be so keen for me to share all my deep and dark secrets with you. And I love you.'

'No,' she denied. 'You don't do love. You don't do commitment.'

'We've had this conversation before. I'm ready to take the risk. With you.'

'But that was before ...'

'Do you really think I'm such a shallow idiot that I could switch off my feelings for you just like that?' He snapped his fingers, eyebrows raised. 'You really have no idea how much I love you, do you?'

'But you were so angry.'

He got up.

'Of course I was angry! I was angry with Pemberton for what he'd done to you, and I was angry with you for refusing to trust me with the truth, and I was angry that it mattered to me so much that you would believe I'd reject you without a fair hearing.'

Laurel stared up at him, hardly able to take it all in.

'You really love me?'

He took her hands in his and brought them to his lips.

'Yes, my sweet Laurel. I love you with all of my heart and soul.'

'But, you don't believe in love, any more than I do.'

'I think you do believe in it, even though you don't trust it. And I realise now I've always believed in it. But I've seen it make fools of so many people. That's what made me so afraid of it too.'

It was too much for her to take in. Panic overwhelmed her and she snatched her hands away.

'Now I know you're winding me up! What is this? Some sort of sick joke? My punishment for not trusting you? Well you can stop it right now! I'm on to you, Daniel French, and I don't like being made a fool of!'

He stood in her path. When she would have turned away he took hold of her shoulders to stop her. She lifted her head and glared at him, her eyes spitting emerald fire. She was like an angry cat and he smiled. Laurel was ready to hit something. *Did he have to find everything she said so amusing? Hadn't the joke gone far enough?*

'I'm the fool,' he told her, suddenly serious. 'A fool for love.'

Laurel closed her eyes and slumped a little. She didn't know how much more of this she could take. When she opened her eyes again the hurt in their depths was clear.

'You still don't believe me,' he said, searching her face.

She wanted to. Oh, how she wanted to!

'Why are you saying these things?' she cried. 'I don't understand what you want!'

He gathered her close, cradling her head against his chest. She was too tired and emotional to fight him.

'Listen to my heart, Laurel. Hear how strong it's beating? Only you can do that to me. When we're apart I can barely function. I want, *I need*, to be by your side when you wake up every morning; to be the father of your children; to put my ring back on your finger – for real this time – and know that it will stay there.'

'But you gave it away,' she reminded him.

Looking sheepish, he took the emerald ring out of his pocket.

'Actually,' he admitted, 'I got it back from Robert in return for a large cash donation.'

'Oh wow! You bought it again? That's so sweet.'

'Will you wear it again, Laurel? If you don't want this one I'll buy you another one, and a wedding ring of course. I want to let the whole world know that you're my love, my heart, my wife. That you'll be mine and I'll be yours, for the rest of our lives.'

'Th ... That's a long time,' she whispered. 'What happened about no commitment? No marriage? No kids?'

'The last gasps of a drowning man.'

'No, you meant it.'

'At first, maybe,' he conceded after a few moments. 'It was certainly true with any other woman. But with you, I don't know. Right from the start I knew you were special. You scared the living daylights out of me. So I fought back, just as you do when you're afraid. Just like you are now.'

'I'm not afraid.'

'You should be, because I'm not about to give up. I may have been afraid of admitting my feelings to begin with, but when I tried to imagine the future without you in my life, that's when I knew what real fear was. I need you

Laurel. You complete me.'

'But I've been to jail. I ...'

'You've done nothing wrong. You've been neglected and abused by the very people who should have protected you. I'm so sorry about that, Laurel.'

She stiffened and he laughed again.

'Don't get all huffy with me. I said I was sorry about it, not sorry for you, woman. Why should I feel sorry for you when you're the bravest, smartest, sweetest person I've ever met?'

Laurel could hardly believe what he was saying. Did she dare believe it? She looked up at him. His gaze was steady and sincere, his eyes almost silver. He stroked her hair.

'My sweet Laurel. I need you so much. Say you'll come home with me? Say you'll stay with me?'

At last Laurel felt that tiny kernel of hope within her bursting through her doubts and knocking them out of its path with the deadly accuracy of a guided missile.

He really loves me! Her heart filled with joy.

'Will you kiss me?' she asked.

'That depends,' he replied, his expression solemn even as his eyes gleamed.

'On what?'

'On whether you're prepared for the fact that I won't be able to stop,' he told her. 'Touching you is addictive. One kiss will never be enough. Only a lifetime of kisses will do.'

'Then you'd better put that ring back where it belongs on my finger, and we'd better get comfortable,' she smiled, taking his hand and leading him into the bedroom.

Women's Contemporary Fiction

For more information about **Alison Rose**

and other **Accent Press** titles

please visit

www.accentpress.co.uk

For news on Accent Press authors and upcoming titles
please visit

http://accenthub.com/

Lightning Source UK Ltd.
Milton Keynes UK
UKOW04f0939151215

264751UK00001B/8/P